Mr O'Brien
Written by Paul Davies

Printed by Book Printing UK

Remus House, Coltsfoot Drive, Peterborough, PE2 9BF

Printed in Great Britain

ISBN: 978-1-3999-2380-4

Monday 10th November

I woke this morning without really knowing who I am. I accidentally wrote the date down wrong by putting an extra digit in it and then I started thinking about 1000 years from now and then, inexplicably, 20 years ago. I felt a little bit lost and when I thought about some other numbers, like the number of people there are, or in fact, how the universe is supposed to be infinite, it made me feel small and irrelevant. It definitely took the shine off me putting the bins out, but I still enjoyed seeing the lorry arrive and the bin go upside down and being emptied. I feel a cleansing finality in it, a renewal, like the bin is having a much-needed, post constipation, empty.

I had looked forward to this day off for weeks but now it's here I realise I have no plan because the beauty of a day off is not to have a plan but now, as I have no plan, I have nothing to do and I'm not hoovering or anything because it's a day off and they are so valuable. I could go shopping but shopping on my own makes me feel self-conscious and I could never try anything on. I also don't want to buy anything as I might have to take it back and I hate that too. When returning absolutely anything at all, they are duty bound to ask invasive questions like 'what's wrong with it?' and they always ask you for your name and address. So, it's best not to bother.

I'll probably have a cup of tea and read for a bit whilst having that nagging feeling of wasting the day. This will be at its strongest when I go to bed without any tiredness and then not sleep. Back at it tomorrow and then I can look forward to my next day off, which is only six short weeks away.

Tuesday 11th November

Back at it today, which means the day starts with the usual bus and a train. Today, in the rain. The train is a more efficient, colder, yet surer experience whilst the bus has more jolts and smiles. I see the same faces pretty much every day and we pull that closed smile face to each other, but we don't *know* each other. It's some sort of acknowledgement that we are fighting out of the same corner. No one I travel with would come to my hospital bed. Why don't we have a chat? We never will. I wonder if they wondered what I was doing yesterday, on my day off. Did they miss me at all? I stopped worrying about what people think of me years ago when I realised how seldom they do. Why does everyone look a bit tired and miserable?

I was thinking about who I am again. If I've changed over the years, then who am I now? And who was I before? and who am I going to be in the future? Am I my brain or does my brain serve me? If I am not my brain, then who am I? I am Mr O'Brien to most people, but who exactly is that? Can I have some, any influence over who I am and who I am going to be or is that for someone or no one else to decide. When I get angry, I just get angry, but why does something make me angry and some other thing not? Are we supposed to be getting something out of this or is it just a random journey through time? Whatever time is.

I've recently read some self-help books but all I could see was how the author was helping himself to my money. Anyway, it's time to get off and make the familiar short walk up to the office. I always steel myself as I enter as if I am to face some sort of test or interrogation. Shoulders back, wide stride.

Wednesday 12th November

Oh, how I hate emails. If in doubt, send an email and cc everyone in you can think of. It's just a way of people writing you a 'to do list' and pushing stuff around. It's like a game of avoidance. Hot potato. I wish people would just *do the thing* and avoid sending the email.

I overreacted today in a meeting. It seemed to be a meeting about meetings. So, I got fed up and asked why we were here. It didn't go down well and it was somewhat out of character for me, but I hardly cared. Maybe I need a new job now, something to give something back, something that actually contributes to improving people's lives. As soon as my share option matures next summer, I'll do that. I probably won't. I am a creature of habit, perhaps brow beaten into submission by 'the system'. I'll keep playing along for a while longer and pretend to myself that I am going to do something about it. I might well be lost without the need to come to this place for eight hours, five days a week

I like it when I feel calm. When I feel life is going my way. I wish I knew why this happened sometimes and so I could feel like that all the time. All I want to do these days is walk and see some nature. Some wildflowers or a bee. That is the height of my ambition now. I can't remember the last time I fought for something I believe in. What do I believe in? Mainly keeping out of the way and a quiet life. I'm not in any race, I am not striving for anything. I even gave up golf as I ran out of people to play with and because I am no good at it. I like books too. So nature and books and maybe cups of tea.

I think I'll have lasagne for dinner.

Thursday 13th November

The amazon delivery was so early today. I decided not to open it, even though I know what it is, just to have that moment after work. I am trying to work out how much I hate my boss and I've decided it is a lot, in fact it is total. So, every time he says something, I am pre-disposed to think what he has just said is stupid. I've decided the next thing he is going to say is also stupid and he hasn't said it yet.

I felt really foolish on the train in to work today as I got so hungry, I decided to have some of my lunch. And then, just before bite one, I dropped it right in the middle of the carriage. Not one bite taken, and it just sat there. I was surprised by an unusual jolt. I went red. People looked out of the corner of their eye. Entertainment. What will he do? Eventually I picked it up and put it in the bin. I felt like Mr Bean not Mr O'Brien. I was still hungry and had less lunch. I was going to buy something for myself but I got put off by everything being described as 'street food'. Who came up with that? Food of the street? It'll pass and I'll pass, thank you.

How close is contentment to boredom? It's a fine line in my opinion. I've also decided I am not very loveable and that I wouldn't really want to be married to me. How do I work on that given I am so comfortable in my own skin, just as I am?

Friday 14th November

Everyone looks forward to Friday and, in particular, Friday afternoon. It's so natural in people. Like they reached the peak of life, but every week. I'm not sure what freedom or excitement it really offers? What amazing things do people do each weekend? I do quite like it too though as I am conditioned by everyone else around me and by the societal norm, but I avoid all the bad feelings people seem to have on a Monday morning, so I feel like I'm making the system work for me. I've no idea what I'll do when I retire. I don't mean in a big way, I mean, on say, a Tuesday morning.

Saturday 15th November

I felt really angry today as the postman shoved and bent my letter when pushing it through the letter box. My letter box has always been a bit on the stiff side, but I felt he could have tried a little harder. The letter had come all that way only to be spoilt at the very end of its journey. *Do not bend*, written in bright red.

Why do we always try to please other people? Like most things, it probably comes from childhood when all we seem to want to do is please our parents and get some sort of meaningless approval. It feels like *everything* at the time. It feels to me like a folly pursuit, so I've decided from now on only to please myself. Who am I kidding?

Sunday 16th November

I went for a walk this morning as the weather was beautifully cold and crisp. As I passed the church, I noticed a large funeral going on. The hearse was just pulling out and there were so many cars, and expensive cars at that. And there were so many beautifully arranged flowers. I couldn't quite make out the name of the deceased. I could hardly get by and I had to step into the road just to make my way. I thought about how loved this newly dead person must have been. It is always such a shame that really popular people don't get to see their big day. Then I thought about my funeral and who might come.

Monday 17th November

I've never understood the phrase 'You are old enough to know better'. Like somehow just not being dead is going to teach you something. I'm not sure how age should alone make you know better. If anything, I'm now old enough to know not to.

Was it Keats who wrote 'Love comes in at the eye', well for most men I know that is not where it stays. Our office is riddled with affairs. I like to play the game of knowing. You can spot them a mile off; they are the ones who try to avoid any eye contact at all. They over try so as not to appear familiar and therefore give the game away. Look closely and you will see their smugness, the tiny knowing look when they say to each other 'Look how clever and naughty we are'. It ends in tears, always.

I had to walk through some right-wing protesters this morning just to get into the office. They were shouting and balling outside some office or other. Their placards were far from clear. Maybe they just wanted to scream and shout for a bit. They were very aggressive though. I do think we need to protest, as that's what brings about true change but it's virtually impossible for me to agree with the far right. To me they look like they are trying to protect something they don't have from a threat that doesn't exist.

Tuesday 18th November

People really moan a lot these days. Some people now have moaning as their default setting. Every meeting I attend seems to start with moaning. Just what do people expect? People really fight with life, when in reality, they have it all. A comfy bed, food aplenty and company, but still they moan and want more. Some brains go unused and are still in their original packaging.

Wednesday 19th November

Our CEO is obsessed with new tech. It's the answer to everything, yet nothing ever really seems to change. We are good at telling the world how great we are. Give a child a hammer and everything becomes a nail. Give a CEO a new buzz word and……….

We seem more interested in how many people read our PR than what we are actually building or doing. I've stopped raising it as they just roll their eyes and say I am out of date. I am not, apparently, 'in the flow'. It's a cycle. Nothing is out of date until everyone can't remember the mistakes that have been made. They'd do well to listen to me from time to time. I am the voice of reason.

Thursday 20th November

I saw on old photo of myself last night when I was clearing up. This is something that might happen less. I mean a real physical old photo. There I was, caught off guard, so not smiling inanely for the camera by request. I'd been caught unknowingly, and it revealed the moment in time. I couldn't think back that far but looking at my face, it made me feel that underneath we change very little. Then I thought about what I'm looking forward to and I couldn't really think of anything that would be good enough to talk about in conversation. I am looking forward to being able to leave work. *Why, what are you going to do then?* I've no idea.

Friday 21st November

The thought that brings me most comfort is to think back from what will be my last day alive. Think back from that day to guide you now. We none of us know how long we have but we act, often, as if we have forever. How would you view, here, right now from the perspective of your final day? I bet I don't wish I'd worked harder. I told this to someone once in the hope that they would find it helpful or maybe even find it mildly profound. But they instantly just said how morbid a thought it was.

I really need to catch up with the washing, I'm running out of socks and I only wear my favourite ones now even though I have seemingly hundreds of pairs.

Saturday 22nd November

Holidays are a mystery to me. Another one of those things that everyone seems to love. They think about them all year but it's not something I've ever really loved or even liked. The trouble is that wherever I go, I am there. I'd like a holiday from myself, but I have to take myself with me. *I'd love a break from me.* Maybe I'll try again as I'd like to find somewhere I could enjoy and somewhere I could look forward to going to. I do like Cornwall. Maybe I could retire down there or maybe buy a second home or a nice static caravan, somewhere I can bolt off to. That would give me something to do and something to look forward to.

Sunday 23rd November

Today I am convinced that not much at all really matters to me. I can say 'So what?' to most anything. *Is that good?*

Monday 24th November

It's my sister's birthday today. She is a bit older than me though you wouldn't think it. She has potions and hair dyes to trick time with whereas I have just let nature have its way. I sent her a card and a text. Job done. We are in no way 'close'.

Someone got locked in the toilet at work today. So now we have to refresh our procedures and have an interim fire drill. In the old days it would have just been funny. I think, in somebody's head or something, the fire drill covers whether someone is locked in a toilet.

Tuesday 25th November

My Mum called me when I got home from work today and I knew that it must mean she needs something fixing or mending. My instinct was right. The boiler won't come on. Now, I know I sound heartless, but she is 70 miles away and through her own choice. She actually chose to move *further away* from me. Anyway, some sort of blood relative guilt kicked in and so I made my way over. It took me three minutes to sort and then I came all the way back. I feel very tired now.

Since Dad passed, I've had a little more communication with my Mum than before. I've never had that mentoring, nurturing or even friendship that others seem to enjoy. You see people whose default action is to 'ring their Mum' and they talk, laugh and cry together. But you can't build a bridge over a vacuum and this vacuum, this abyss, has been the norm for too many a year.

Wednesday 26th November

I was very bored at work today and so I made a list today of all the addresses I've ever lived at. There are only three, so then I made a list of all my lovers and there are only two of them. I made the lists into one list to make it look big enough to be a list. And then I stared at it and realised there are probably no more entries to be added to it now. *Probably, he says.*

Thursday 27th November

Christmas is in full swing now. I apparently offended someone in the office today by calling it Christmas. I really didn't mean to. I don't think I actually offended anyone directly, but it was pointed out that I should be careful as I *might* offend someone. That's just what I've always called it. Live and let live, I say. I'm not really religious anyway. On that front, I don't even know what I'm hoping for.

I have mixed feelings about Christmas. It's some time off to relax but it also provokes a sadness for me now that I am on my own. I know it was my choice and there are days when I do wish I hadn't killed her but mostly I'm glad I did. It was for the best. Like when you see an animal half dead on the road, and you decide to run it over to end its misery. I think sometimes the memory of someone is an enhanced version of the reality they brought. All dead people are great, aren't they? Towards the end it was all just too painful for us both. *Well, for me.*

Friday 28th November

My life is pretty comfortable when I come to think about it. It's pretty easy, but I do wonder sometimes who would come to my hospital bed if I was really ill or I if I'd had an accident. I'm not sure my Mum would make it or even bother to try.

My boss has a private number plate. Who has a private number plate? And why? Anyone who has a private number plate is putting their happiness in the hands of others. *Look at me, I have a private number plate!* What a total waste of money. *Look at me, I'm totally insecure and need you to be impressed!* Well, I suppose everyone is a teacher. Everyone can teach us something even if it is how not to be. That's how I think of my Dad.

Saturday 29th November

Today I did some of those odd jobs that need doing but that never feel like a priority. After that I did dusting, cleaning and hoovering which gave me a sense of satisfaction and the feeling that I had earned some sort of reward.

My house felt in order and this gave me a pleasant feeling all evening.

Sunday 30th November

I wasted today and didn't do anything that I should have or am supposed to.

Monday 1st December

I was forced to attend a work meeting today called 'The Town Hall'. A 'three line whip' apparently. Why do people, particularly in work environments, peddle such bullshit. The idea is we get to see an overview of where the company is and then we feel more motivated and clear on what we are doing. They should have called it 'The Cliché Hall'. I've never heard so much tripe being rolled out. One after the other, they just rolled of the tongue and appeared on the PowerPoint. The fancy graphics and wavy lines were something to behold but my goodness, the muck spreader was working hard. Work harder and earn someone else even more money. Work harder but your pay isn't going up, it will just make the owners richer. *What do they think we are, stupid?* My favourite cliché was 'The traffic is thinner in the extra mile'. Well actually, as I pointed out, that is counter intuitive, as if you are asking us *all* to work harder then we will all be going the extra mile. The silence was both pleasing and deafening.

I only work as I'd feel guilty if I didn't. Well, that and the money. Nobody is truly fooling anybody else of anything. If you don't believe me then let's see who will work for free, I said.

Tuesday 2nd December

Someone at work mentioned imposter syndrome to me today. Apparently, it is all to do with believing you are not worthy nor deserving of your status or achievements. Initially it felt like an odd concept to me as I have always believed I missed my calling, my purpose, and in some way I was indeed destined for a higher plane. Then I thought about all of those people who seem to fall upwards and actually should be suffering from this but it seems it is not them, it is the good and worthy people, doubting themselves for their advancements and achievements. I mean, who in their right mind could ever think, for example, that they were destined to be, say, *President of the United States.* So, in the end, I think I understood it. Only us humans could suffer from such a thing. It reminded me of Charles Bukowski when he said that the problem with the world is that all the intelligent people are full of doubts whilst the stupid ones are full of confidence.

I tried meditation today after work. I've tried before and it is harder than I thought it would be. Just sitting still and thinking of nothing. Were we designed for that? *What animal is designed for that?* It took me a little while to clear my mind and then I fell asleep, which was really nice, but then I was groggy and couldn't get back to sleep at night so all in all not a huge success.

Wednesday 3rd December

I do miss her sometimes, but it soon passes. Mum called again today to try and organise Christmas. It took about fifteen minutes and fourteen of those were her apologising that she is going to her friend's house for Christmas dinner. I am to go and see her on the 27th as that's when she can fit me in. No point getting presents this year she says, as she doesn't want or need anything at her age. I surely have to get her something, don't I?

Thursday 4th December

I thought a bit about death today. I reckon we all do at times. It is necessary, isn't it? I mean without it we would go on forever and nothing would really matter or ever seem truly urgent. It's only when something is scarce that it is valuable. I tried to be positive about what I can do with my remaining days and I tried to work how many of them there might be. I reckon I've got less than ten thousand now and that's if I am really lucky. I couldn't think of much I wanted to achieve but it did prompt me to order a new mattress.

Friday 5th December

As someone once famously said, 'The days are long, but the years are short'. I thought about my relationship with my Mum again today. I'm not sure why she ever wanted children. She had one and then, inexplicably, decided to have another. Maybe after one she wanted to try again to see if she could get it right or maybe she had forgotten what it was like the first time. Or maybe both or the second one was a mistake. Maybe it was just the thing to do. I think she wanted *a child* maybe, but not *this child*. She didn't choose to have *me*, she chose to have *a child* that turned out to be me so maybe there's no reason at all for us to like each other or stay in touch. There's certainly no way I signed up to be a carer for her and I worry a bit that this is where it is heading. How was that ever the deal? Babies can't make deals, and now this is where I am. Somewhat cornered.

Saturday 6th December

My surname causes so many issues with technology. It's a very simple name but because it starts with 'O apostrophe', it causes me no end of annoyance. I didn't choose it and my email addresses have no apostrophe in them. I decided to look it up as I never really knew what it meant. It is Gaelic for 'descendent of Brian'. How very exciting. How come Brian, at that point in history, got to stamp his authority on everyone's name forever after. I hope he was worth it and that he was a good man. I somehow doubt it. At least it explains my native Irish grandparents, but of course, we never speak about them, and I can barely remember them. Maybe I'll research my family tree. It's easier nowadays. Are all O'Brien's descendants of the same Brian or were there lots of Brian's all at one time who got together and decided to assert the surname on generations to come? I bet that meeting was in the pub. I'd like to have been there and raised a glass with all the Brian's.

Sunday 7th December

I read in the newspaper today about the rise of 'AI' and its impact on humanity. I worry about climate change and now of course pandemics, so it's lovely to complete a set. Now I have three things to keep me awake. I can do something about all three though and so I will do my bit and try not to worry so much. Maybe the first thing I'll do is stop buying a newspaper as that's a double win, firstly it will save paper and secondly, I won't have to read about stuff like this again.

I think we ignore two truly fundamental truths. One is that there are too many of us, too many humans that is, and two, we don't seem to understand the limit of our own human intelligence. Our arrogance (which is proof of the limitation) allows to believe we are not only the highest rung on the food chain but indeed we are as intelligent as anything could ever be. We can't be that clever, can we? Just look around. And also, we are not at the end of evolution or time, just at a point on the journey. One day every bit of this will be seen as incredibly old fashioned and then it will all be forgotten.

I love to walk, and I love to see others walking, particularly with their dogs. Dogs always seem so giving and they seem so easily pleased and happy in the moment. They must be a real fillip for their owners. I thought about getting one, but I don't think I could handle the mess, the cleaning up and the dirtiness. Shame. I'll just walk on my own with my thoughts. I've also found loads of places to hide or to dispose of things, should I ever need to.

Monday 8th December

It was freezing today. The bus and train felt so cold after the weekend.

We really are the result of our battles, aren't we? So why do we fear the next one so much? I wouldn't change a thing. In my view, battle scars are better than certificates, both the physical and the mental ones.

How come I have to write more Christmas cards each year, yet I've got less people in my life? It crossed my mind that I might be sending cards to dead people. How would I ever know? They can't write back and let me know, can they? How long after I am dead will I receive Christmas cards and when and from whom will be the very last one?

Tuesday 9th December

I do get quite anxious sometimes and I don't know why. I sometimes wake up in the middle of the night with my stomach turning over and feeling tight and horrible. A long walk in the cold air always helps. That and organising my thoughts a little. I know others struggle with this far more than I do, and I feel truly sorry for them and wish I could help. I might try meditation again. I could never go to the doctor. *What would I say?* I'd just be wasting his time.

Wednesday 10th December

Have you noticed those people that say, 'Is there anything I can do?' but they say it in a way that really means 'I don't want to do anything at all really.' They offer nothing, they don't even take responsibility for the help they are not really even trying to give. They say things like 'Keep an eye on it' or 'Maybe you should do something about it.' I hate those people. They are pretending to help without ever really wanting to get involved or to even think fully about how they might be able to help. But they sleep at night believing they did something to assist. I hate them and it covers a lot of people. Most people, I would say.

Thursday 11th December

I really have become one of life's passengers, haven't I? But then, how many people who have ever lived, as a percentage, have ever really done or changed anything? It's very few I think, and I admire them greatly as they often had to sacrifice much or even all of their own life to bring about the change they believed in. I wonder if I would do the same and I wonder if circumstance was a factor in them being 'the one'. I just don't think that moment ever came for me. I've never felt that strongly or ever saw such an opportunity or need.

'Settling down' is really a wonderful thing. 'Settling for' is not. I've done both.

Friday 12th December

An unusually sunny winters day coupled with the promise of Christmas seemed to give everyone at work and on the bus and train a pleasant disposition. I tried to join in on that as much as I could.

Saturday 13th December

I thought today, when on my walk, where I am on two different axis. Firstly, if I live to an average age, which Google says is about 80, then where am I on my life's timeline. Secondly, I then thought about where I am compared to everyone else on the planet. So, there are billionaires and a fair few others above me, but there are billions more below me. Both thoughts gave me some sort of calming effect and I tried to imagine one crossed line graphic to plot myself on, but then I gave up as my favourite table outside my favourite café was free and there was nobody else around. So I sat and had a coffee and a bagel in the cold air, and it was wonderful.

Sunday 14th December

The films and books that you watch and read twice or more are your real favourites.

Monday 15th December

A heavy frost this morning again which felt somehow purifying, as if the streets and the outside are having a much needed clean. The slippiness underfoot a reminder of our fragility in the world. As a species we really do strut around as if we own the place. We would do well to remind ourselves of life's fine balance more often.

A hot coffee at the station brought much joy and I was lucky enough to just stare at a tree for five minutes. Trees are so patient. I wondered how and when it decided to shed its leaves this year and then I wondered why it is at its barest when the world is at its coldest. I look forward to seeing the renewal in spring, the sunshine, and the brand-new leaves of green.

Work really does get in the way. Meetings are a curse only second to emails. 'Let's have a meeting'. Most of them don't seem to come to much at all but really, what do I care? Pay day is the same every month whether I go or not. I saw a few snowflakes dropping outside the window and it was really hard not to just turn round and watch them gracefully descend to their death as they each landed on the wet, salted road.

I somehow enjoyed the journey home in the dark and the feeling of arriving home. All in all, for no reason I can quite understand, a good day.

Tuesday 16th December

She was in the office today. How lovely she is and how lovely that she seems completely unaware of the fact. I always try not to over manufacture a meeting or a conversation with her, but then fate intervened in a beautiful way. I just wandered into the kitchen to make a drink and there she was, looking for coffee, as we had run out. Opening and closing each door and cupboard with a grace at home on a stage. A prolonged stay beckoned and an easy way to create small talk was offered. I tried to get the balance right and I made her smile, almost laugh, and we chatted and it was as easy as a morning spring breeze. I lost myself within the conversation at one point and had to regain some focus as I had no idea what I was saying. I was so pleased with myself and left casually before she did. *How very cool of me.* In my simple head, I had created a need for more in her. I enjoyed believing this for a few minutes. At the end of the day, she seemed to make a special effort to say goodbye. Eye contact, a smile and one of those cute little waves that people do now. I longed to follow her out, to tell her how beautiful she is, but of course I never could. I can't remember anything else about today, only that.

Wednesday 17th December

The office talk is solely about the Christmas doo on Friday night. It now, inexplicably, seems okay to call it Christmas, but I didn't say the word. Why can't people see it for what it is? Heavy drinking, the distraction of food, bad dancing, corny music, late to bed followed by a hangover and perhaps some shame for a selected few. I didn't go last year but it was noticed, so I sort of have to go this year. We have to sit on random tables this year which is good for me as I am not really in any group as such so it saves me the embarrassment of the outsider. I bet the office all hope they don't have to sit next to me. It reminds me of being picked last at team sports in school, which I sometimes was. *Just maybe I'll be sitting next to her though.* Fate could never be that kind.

Thursday 18th December

I worked from home today, so had the luxury of a lovely long walk at lunchtime on a familiar route. The rain had abated for the day and so I went out early as I couldn't wait nor resist the allure of the crisp and frosted pavements. There is no bad weather, only bad clothes. I noticed just how much people tend to their properties, their mini territories. Fixing and improving their lawns and fences, sweeping, even cleaning their cars meticulously. Every little weed removed on the space they call 'theirs'. Yet just a few strides away you find litter on the streets and people sitting in idling cars with engines on whilst scrolling on phones. How have we become so entrenched in our little plots of land and forgotten we are all part of a bigger, entwined picture? All we each need to do is to extend just a little bit further outwards and we'd change the world. That's all it would take. We are a society and we are dependent upon eco-systems, both natural and man-made, working in harmony for our happiness and even our very survival. There's no point tending to your lawn when the water is lapping up to your door.

Friday 19th December

All I really want is to stay in bed all day. At least, that's what I think I want when I first wake up. But that's not what I really want. I have no idea what I really want. Who does?

Saturday 20th December

The Christmas doo was so stereotypically 'the Christmas doo' it was almost a parody of itself. So cliche. Firstly nerves, then food, then drink, inhibition, then more drink, embarrassment, some real fools and the sobering cold air whilst waiting for a taxi. I am simply an observer of it all. I went unnoticed. I looked for her, I saw her, she looked so beautiful, and we had a brief conversation. So, it was worth it.

Sunday 21st December

I started and concluded my Christmas shopping today and I posted the cards I have chosen to send. One of the advantages of having a smaller life than most is that this Christmas shopping is a truly manageable task within a couple of hours. I did end up getting my Mum something. I got *her* something too, but I doubt I'll get the chance to give it to her.

I put a tree up of sorts and some lights today. Just to join in.

Monday 22nd December

I am not sure I am the most courageous of individuals. I am more of the silent type rather than someone who might intervene and bring about change. I'm not sure if I've just given up, or maybe I am just a bit shy and reserved or am I just feeling my age? Experience has taught me that I can't seem to change all that much, plus I don't really feel the passionate burn that seems to consume others. So, I do ask myself at times, what is my purpose here?

Tuesday 23rd December

Snow fell today whilst I was on my way to work and it got heavier and heavier. Apart from the mild worry that transport would cease, it drove some of my colleagues to build snowmen and throw snowballs at each other during lunch time. Strangely I enjoyed watching this and wanted to join in but could never do so without due invitation. So, I just found myself watching and smiling a bit and then I made a nice coffee and watched some more. She went outside with a beautiful long winter coat on. She seemed to want to join in but then something stopped her. She just stood at the edge of the frivolity and clasped her hands. I caught her eye and she offered a meek half wave, which I returned.

Wednesday 24th December

I was one of the 'volunteers' to go into work today and do the half day that is required of a few of us. It's a nice day in my view and everyone is in good spirits. Plus, I wouldn't want to waste a precious holiday day. She wasn't in, so my last chance, my best chance to secretly give her the present I had for her has passed. I'm not sure I would have been brave, or forward enough anyway. *What will I do with it now?*

The train home was almost empty.

Thursday 25th December

Uneventful.

Friday 26th December

I'm getting ready to see my mother tomorrow. I've spent too much of today getting ready for something that needs no real preparation, so I have concluded that I am bored. I tried not to think of too many others today and what they might be doing. I found myself tidying the garage but it's way too cold and too big a job so I just felt irritable. Too much time on my own can be a good thing and sometimes, in equal measure, a bad thing.

People hold such strange truths, in fact, it seems, everyone holds their own truths in which they have complete and utter conviction. In my view, the stronger the conviction, the more you need to question it. But just what is the truth, and does it even exist outside the mind?

Saturday 27th December

A long frosty drive, a present for Mum, but true to her word, nothing for me in return. Some cold food on a paper plate and then a long frosty drive back in the dark. No love at all. Very transactional.

A waste of time but I had nothing better to do. *I can play the long game.* Just as long as I am a major beneficiary in the will. I am owed.

Sunday 28th December

I have to make the most of today as it's back to work tomorrow. I'll be glad when the weather is warmer and daylight is longer so I'm looking forward to spring. To see all around me springing back into life.

Monday 29th December

Back to work today. She is not in, and I expected her to be, though I am not entirely sure why. I am sure she was meant to be in, but I cannot ask or check. I cannot seem outwardly interested.

It's a shame the only real way humans can communicate is through words. Imagine if we could just plug into each other like computers and pass on thoughts, feelings and experiences in a much purer way. Perhaps even a new system where only the truth can be passed. The world is designed to be against those who are not good with words. This world is for the salesmen, this world is for good liars. I hate them. Them and their silver tongues and their manipulation.

Tuesday 30th December

Another year is about to end and for some reason we are all going to celebrate that and make a big deal of welcoming in a new one. We kid ourselves that this creates some sort of blank canvas. It doesn't. We drag along our past and our complicated minds and our ageing bodies through each year after the last like huge sacks of dirt we cannot detach. Like Sisyphus, we just keep on pushing all that baggage uphill. No blank canvas. New year is a trick of the calendar. Although, having said that, this will be the first year that I start completely on my own as a widow. I prefer 'as a single man' I think as it sounds a bit younger or maybe just a bit more acceptable.

The guilt won't leave me though just because a page turns. Maybe it's not guilt, more just a feeling that I have not been careful enough and left a tiny trace of something, somewhere, somehow.

Wednesday 31st December

I've come to dislike New Years Eve quite considerably. I didn't mind it so much when I was younger but now, somehow, I feel at a loose end and somewhat edgy and restless. And then nothing at all much happens and I'll watch the fireworks on the BBC and go to bed. So what?

Thursday 1st January

The frosty weather yet again had a cleansing quality that seems perfectly in line with the first day of a new year. I went for a long walk and enjoyed the views of trees, fields and water. Although not much other life crossed my path. The water looked so very cold, freezing and it made me shudder to think about being in it. I pulled my coat up to my chin and walked home a little quicker than I walked there. I thought about how horrible it must be to be homeless, especially at this time of year. The physical struggle alone must be immense but that coupled with the mental battle must make it a terrible and depressing way to live. If it is living at all. I'll give something to a homeless charity tomorrow. I was certainly pleased to get in and make a warm drink.

Friday 2nd January

I woke up thinking of the funeral today. Just somehow, I couldn't get it out of my head. I've not really had this before, but it kept waking me like some sort of gentle yet evil bedfellow prompting me to consider what is gone, what is behind me. Why can't our minds just leave things be or indeed stop stressing about what is to come. Being in bed is my favourite place in the world so why won't my troublesome brain just let me be. My body loves bed but my mind can sometimes try to spoil it. I thought about the lead up to it, the weeks and months before and how it all came to pass. I thought a lot about what I had done but mainly the day of the funeral itself when everyone dressed in black and bowed heads and expressed sadness and pity towards me. Not that huge numbers came. We were never big on being social or pushing outwards. We used to just love each other's company and then less so. My fondest memories are of us both just sitting there, reading books in total silence. Taking turns to bring a hot drink and maybe a snack or biscuit. Just being happy in each other's company without having to talk all the time. Sometimes we would recommend books to each other or talk a bit about chapters or passages that really made us feel something. *Where did all that go?*

It didn't feel much like a Friday in work today and I'm sort of glad she wasn't in today after my restless night and thoughts of early morning. I was unsettled, unsettled by the calendar I think.

Saturday 3rd January

What to do on a day like today? Nothing, that's what.

Sunday 4th January

I considered buying a new car today, given the new year and the feeling of a fresh start. It soon passed though as I tried to navigate the internet. Now I'll be bothered with adverts for cars for the next fifty years whenever I go online. The machines are learning, so teach them well and, most of all, be kind.

Monday 5th January

The distraction of work returned today and it has made me feel less lost and more normal. Plus, she was back in today, but looking more than just a little bit sad, upset even. I mean, still incredibly beautiful, fascinating and irresistible but a little sullen perhaps. I didn't manage to speak to her, but I feel buoyed to know there will be many and multiple opportunities on the way now that we are all back to normal.

Tuesday 6th January

I knew something was brewing at work and today most of us were delivered a letter in an envelope. Yes, an actual typed letter in an actual window envelope. How incredibly Victorian. Of course, this can only mean one thing, we are having another restructure and it appears that I have to re-apply for my own job. Again. Who on earth came up with such a thing? Surely, they already know if I can do my own job and how well. I have been doing it for years. They will already know who is for the chop. There is a list, a spreadsheet somewhere with a red line on it. My fate has already been set. One thing is for sure, there is going to be less of us so that they can make even more money for the already rich. Capitalism at its very best. Soft words justify everything these days. 'Streamlining', 'efficiencies', 'unavoidable'. This plan of action is not just for the best but apparently 'inevitable'. The redundancy package is lucrative given my years of service so that provides food for thought and room for some potential mischief. I don't very much like my job but I've no idea what I'd do without it or how I'd get another one. I'd probably not much like any new job either.

Wednesday 7th January

I spoke to her again today, just briefly and in the kitchen. There is something giving her sadness and I so want to help. Maybe it's the redundancy letter, but I doubt it. For a start, she'll fly through the process like she always does. How could anyone ever consider sending her away? On the way home all my brain could do for me was to recite Yeats' 'Wine comes in at the mouth/Love comes in at the eye/That's all we shall know for truth/Before we grow old and die/I lift my glass to my mouth/I look at you and I sigh'. Over and over and over and each time it went around in my head I felt my heart gently break.

Thursday 8th January

I saw her again today and I'm finding it hard not to fix my gaze, to stare at her almost permanently. I imagine how awful it would look if she, or anyone else, thought I was staring at her. It is difficult though as she is so graceful, so beautiful. I don't want her to think I am some sort of oddball. I need to keep a strong sense of decorum.

Friday 9th January

Lady luck was smiling on me today, but I also feel guilty for feeling lucky given it feels like it is at her misfortune.

I saw her in the kitchen with her colleague and she was being consoled as they looked at her phone. Those tiny screens are evil, they make you addicted to something you're not even enjoying. Anyway, I asked if there was anything I could do and was genuinely concerned. This must have come across well as later on she came to speak to me. Yes, she actually came to speak to me and we had a chat. It seems her relationship has ended. I don't know any of the details, but I couldn't help but think about the fact that she is now single. I'm not sure what I am supposed to think or whether this makes me a bad person, but I did feel some happiness and then I realised I'd never have the confidence or bravery to ask anything of her and that made me feel sad again. I think I said something totally corny and sickly, along the lines of 'how could anybody not want to be with you' and she looked kind of dazed but complimented and I immediately regretted it and then didn't. It was very awkward for a second or two. I told her that if she wanted to talk, I'd really listen and we could perhaps go for coffee. That's about the bravest I've ever been. I wanted to hug her but that just wouldn't have been right or in any way appropriate. She said I was a good friend. What progress has been made today! *A friend! A good friend even!* I didn't know she even ever thought about me. I'm not sure at all what to do next but imagine just her and I even just going for a coffee. I'll have to see how things are over the next few days, but I shouldn't miss this opportunity. On the way home I thought about it all and then I imagined that they will simply get back together in a few days and, by the middle of next week everything will be as it was. She'll have forgotten the whole thing, including me being a friend and our coffee.

I am rambling somewhat.

Saturday 10th January

I really should call my mother, but I just can't be bothered. In the end I did and was right to have concluded that I indeed shouldn't have bothered. I think I interrupted her somehow and she seemed irritated. She asked me about the opening times at Ikea. No warmth either way. Sometimes family ties are just that and nothing else. Binding, god given and of no value.

Sunday 11th January

I woke up this morning really early, too early, which is always annoying when you have the chance to stay in bed a little longer. I was thinking back to last year, to being married, before it all happened. My mind played tricks on me and that made me feel guilty and lonely in excess, when, in truth, I'm only a little bit of either. I reminded myself that my life is much more serene and settled now. I couldn't get back to sleep after all that thought and so in the end, I made a coffee and stared out of the window. I saw a little robin just sitting and bobbling along on the fence. How did he not feel the cold? How did such a little bird seem to look so content, even happy? He made me smile and then he bobbed off again up a tree. After my coffee I realised I have nothing at all to do today really and so I went for a walk. The other things I could imagine doing, I really didn't want to do. I managed about five miles before I had the feeling of wanting to be home and so the trick was complete and I came home, had a cup of tea, had a look out for the robin and then put the television on and fell asleep. How would I assess this day out of ten? Eight probably.

Monday 12th January

I battled to put the recycling bin out this morning due to a strong storm. Strong enough to have been given a name on TV and some sort of cosy, short-lived celebrity status. Bits of all sorts were blowing everywhere across the street, and I hope my bin is collected before it blows over. Mine is quite light, very rarely anywhere near full, so could go over in a flash. I tried to push the waste down a bit, to create a solid base, but there was nothing particularly heavy, just a few cartons, newspapers and bottles and the like. I'm not sure my neighbours, or others, are quite appreciative of the irony of trying to put your recycling out in such conditions. I also noticed just how overflowing everyone else's bin seemed to be. Just what are they doing, just what are they buying all the time?

We all arrived at work today with further communication awaiting us in our inboxes. *How exciting.* Some poor sod or other from HR must have been working on the weekend to organise the interviews for people who already hold the jobs. It seems everyone got one, so it is clear to me that people who are already leaving, or should I say, are being sacked with a pay-off, are being put through the ringer and stress of an interview they cannot possibly be successful in. That is just not fair. Some people desperately want to stay, and others want to leave but want the maximum pay out, and so it has become a game. Some people pretend they want to leave but anxiously want to stay. No honesty and no hands going up. Chess. My 'interview process' is on the 21st and I have a short presentation to prepare along with a statement and then there will be questions from 'the panel'. The macabre side of me is quite looking forward to it. I cannot lose really. As long as we *both* get the same result, I'll be happy.

Tuesday 13th January

I do love listening to music, but I much prefer to hear it out loud. I've never really taken to headphones. I hate that buzzing noise that other people's headphones make. I once read something by Alan Watts that said that life is like a song or a piece of music and we should enjoy it as it plays rather than fixating on its ending, which is what we often tend to do in life. We do spend so much time thinking about what's to come and what has been. The moment in time where we are does seem so fleeting and difficult to concentrate on. Time is somewhat confusing and muddling.

It's hard to find time to cook properly during the week and I do worry I don't eat enough or healthily enough. But, like most things, it passes and I do get by alright.

Wednesday 14th January

Panic is setting in at the office. Everyone is trying to work out what everyone else is doing for the interviews. It's like the FBI and everyone should have those camel raincoats on and fedoras. It reminds me of school and homework but with more at stake. I'm playing it so cool that people are beginning to suspect I know something that I most certainly do not, which is quite fun. People are looking tired and stressed. It's as understandable as it is unnecessary. Why not just tell them now who is staying and who is leaving?

Thursday 15th January

We really do feel we are the centre of the world and we seem to treat people as if they are there solely here to make our lives easier. You might be the central character in your own movie but there are billions of other movies going on, most of which you do not appear in.

Friday 16th January

I wish I could take some time off from being me. Just a few days. I imagine I am tiring to be with. I do find myself tyring.

Saturday 17th January

It's such a long time since we have all been paid. Money does make the world go round for many people. I am very lucky to be comfortable and have realised that money doesn't make you happy, it simply removes discomfort and gives you more choice. I never fell into the trap of buying things just because I could or to try and make myself happy so I've saved up for no real reason. Some people buy things just to show them to other people. How stupid does that sound? If I listed the things that make me happy, things I could buy wouldn't make the top ten. I wish the robin would pop back.

Sunday 18th January

Working on a Sunday, I ask you. I finally got the motivation from somewhere to do my prep for next week and I nailed it in a half hour or so. I am happy to play a game where I cannot lose. I actually think my presentation will be really good so maybe, if I am on the hit list, that will make them think twice. Do I want that? I'm not sure but there is some sort of competitive element in me somewhere that says I must nail this. *How bizarre.*

I felt like I wanted to plant a tree today, but it passed. If we all just planted two trees, that would make a world of difference.

Monday 19th January

I watched a debate on television this evening where some government minister or other was trying to defend the fact that the 'defence budget' had to be cut and some army chief or other was explaining why it needed to be bigger. What struck me was why they call it a 'defence' budget. In my view it's an 'attack' budget. Who ever heard of a weapon of defence?

Tuesday 20th January

Interview eve for many. She came and asked me for help today. She wanted me to look over her preparation which is against the office norm, but who cares about that? Her prep was perfection itself and I actually stole a point or two from hers for mine. I reassured and added some small pearls of wisdom and she seemed happy. We are both in a better position for the conversation and it was so lovely just to engage. And then, and then, somehow, we arranged to go for a coffee straight after work a week on Wednesday. Some sort of debrief or post interview discussion, but whatever it is I can barely hide my excitement of being one on one with her for about an hour. *Will it be an hour?* And it was her idea. What does she think of me? I'll try not to overthink it too much so that I don't turn into a bumbling idiot. What a week this is turning out to be.

Wednesday 21st January

The queen was on television last night. It's hard not to have some respect for her, not least because she has allowed herself to become 'The queen'. Not just 'A queen', but 'The queen', as if no other queens exist or are as worthy of the title. So, respect for that. I might call myself 'The Mr O'Brien' from now on, or maybe just 'The O'Brien' and see how that goes down. To be fair to her, it probably wasn't of her doing.

The interview seemed to go well. I can play the game, I can act up to what is required. I felt in control and they nodded a lot, too much.

Thursday 22nd January

The communication at work has been awful as nobody is quite clear regarding what will happen next or quite when and so the rumour mill and gossip engines are in overdrive. I keep reminding people that what is done is done now and there's nothing they can do about it, and they keep reminding me just how much this matters to them. Apart from the ones pretending not to care. It's not quite life and death but it seems to be livelihood or poverty for quite a few. So dramatic. There are other jobs. The fear of them losing their jobs is seemingly disproportionately immense. The fear is in your head.

Less than a week until 'coffee' now.

Friday 23rd January

I wondered today if the robin was in fact my wife. But then I realised how silly a thought this was. But why did I even think it? I mean I suppose it could be but, the chances are tiny. If it is it is a good job it cannot talk.

We have been told today that the HR process 'should be concluded by the end of next week'. They have something to think about or, at least, they need to give off the illusion of a proper, full process.

Saturday 24th January

I allowed myself to think about receiving redundancy and what that would mean for me. It's a big amount of money. At the beginning my thoughts were positive. Money, free time, what's not to like, but then I worried what might happen if I had nothing to do and no one to see. What would I do all day? That worried me more than the happiness of leaving so I guess I am hoping I'll keep my job. I'm only putting off then inevitable though as I'll have to retire one day. I should prepare. I should do some research.

All the sport was cancelled today due to the bad weather and the world of television acted as if it was the end of the world and the cessation of all human civilisation.

Sunday 25th January

I hope coffee is still on with her on Wednesday, otherwise I might as well just be dead.

I thought about ringing my mother today and then my sister but thankfully the feeling passed.

Monday 26th January

Today was better than any of the weekend days as I spoke to her in the kitchen. This is our place to engage for now. She smiled as she saw me and that made my heart just glow. I smiled back totally instinctively. How beautiful she is when she smiles. Totally beautiful, as if there is nothing else to think about in the world. She was wearing a lovely dress, so simple, so elegant. We chatted and confirmed our coffee for Wednesday. She apologised in advance for her habit of talking too much. *Please, talk as much as you can, let me see your lips moving and your eyes darting, full of message and intent.*

Tuesday 27th January

There is no need to cling so hard. Everything is temporary, everything is essentially rented for a relatively short space of time. There is no need to cling to things, like you do. No need at all. We all just want to be happy. Let your death guide you, be your companion and do not die before you die.

Wednesday 28th January

This was one of the best days of my life. I cannot even remember work. But I'll never forget our coffee. The setting was perfect. I had worried it would be too busy, but it wasn't. The coffee was hot and the barista was attentive but not intrusive. She sat, she talked, she laughed. I barely said a word. I just took it all in. She was sad because her relationship ended on New Year's Eve. This gave me pleasure but then immediate guilt regarding that pleasure. She is going to focus in on work now she says. She hopes to keep her job and thinks she will but doesn't want to be over confident about it. She didn't really ask about me, but I didn't care. I haven't got anything to say anyway. I wanted to tell her that I love her, but it would have been totally disproportionate and stupidly early, so I simply couldn't. *But I do.* I did manage to say that I liked her coat. At the end I almost felt a kiss coming. A peck on the cheek, not a romantic or prolonged kiss but awkward me had no idea what to do or quite when. We exchanged numbers which was just glorious. I'll think about this for as long as my memory lasts. I have her number. *Note to self, don't start texting her all the time.* Do I love her? It's easy to convince myself that I do but do I, can I, already?

Thursday 29th January

I simply cannot bear it when I tear a page out of my notebook and it doesn't tear cleanly. When it pulls beyond the perforations taking some of the margin paper with it. It spoils both the page I've torn out and the notebook itself then looks so scruffy. I waste time making it good. I always try to repair and sort, but it is unbearable. Unbearable.

Friday 30th January

I'm devastated as I write this. And I have no idea what to do but I am so angry and frustrated and helpless. I have been rewarded with my own job. It was offered to me like a shiny new car or some sort of gameshow star prize. Modern life is ridiculous. It was mine already. But she, my darling, is being made redundant. How on gods earth, or any earth, can they be letting her go when they have her here each day. She is brilliant, she is perfect. She was inconsolable. The office was a cooking pot of high emotion as people cried and were comforted by the ones who had beat them to their jobs. The company created this, all in the name of making more money. In the ensuing melee I didn't speak to her. I didn't even really see her. I'd give my job up for her to stay but the point is that we are there together. What can be done? How can this have happened now. How? I'm devastated.

I sent her a text offering help and support, but no answer yet. *Are you okay my darling?*

Saturday 31st January

Still no reply to my text. I've composed hundreds of others but sent none. I stare at my sent message a lot in an attempt to induce a reply, like Derren Brown might, but unlike him, I fail. *Please reply my darling, I can think of nothing else.*

Sunday 1st February

A new month but I don't care. No fresh start. New months should not begin on a Sunday.

In the mid-afternoon my phone pinged. It gave me a start as it rarely makes a noise, and I was pleased to see it was her reply. 'Thank you so much, you are so lovely. I'm not sure what to do. See you tomorrow x'. I've read it a thousand times. She says I'm lovely, she's confused, she will see me tomorrow. *I'll be there for you, always, my darling.*

Monday 2nd February

I received a call from my sister late last night. For some reason she felt the need to tell me she is due in hospital today. It's a family thing, I think, where we have to pretend we care, or maybe, more accurately, where we are duty bound to care rather than caring by any sort of choice. She mentioned she needs blood and then asked me if I gave blood. I was cornered but the truth is I don't, but I probably should. It made me think that it is a good job that blood groups exist and that it is not like fingerprints, where we each have our unique type. If we did, we would then certainly all give blood and store some aside for ourselves, just in case we needed it.

Tuesday 3rd February

I only saw my love later on yesterday. The hurt of this process has opened her up to me in new ways. She is clinging to me a little bit more now. It is a splendid development in an awful situation. She has a bigger enemy and that has brought us closer. This tends to be the way in life. She needs me and whilst I absolutely love that, I'm still angry that our time at work together is ticking down. There seems to be nothing either of us can do to reverse that. It feels like a death of sorts but I need to turn this into the birth of fuller us. I have offered support but that sounds so crass. *Support, I ask you.* I'm not brave enough to offer my love, but she can have it all in an instant.

Wednesday 4th February

Last night I looked at a naked woman on the internet. I shouldn't have done it but now I am being bombarded with similar and I feel like a pervert, which I am not. We are fast becoming lab rats for the machines. The rewards are constantly dangled. The things we 'need'. The prize is a lie. It's just 'sales'. We are the rat, or the donkey and the carrot is always just within reach but never within reach. It's not about the donkey or the carrot, it's about who or what is controlling the stick. I've never been one for porn. My brain looks at it and tries to assess the 'actors' back stories and I can't help feeling sorry for the women, like they don't really want to be there and they are being taken advantage of. I've no idea if that is true but I can't imagine many little girls dreaming of such a career, so it makes me feel sad. This is not something I have ever, can ever discuss but I somehow sincerely doubt that many other men think like me, otherwise the whole industry wouldn't be so popular.

Her date for leaving is the end of March. I have just under two months to ensure we do not lose touch, to ensure there is a chance for us.

Thursday 5th February

I have not heard from my sister and I have a strange feeling that I hope she is okay, maybe even that I care. Do I text? Do I just wait? I feel a bit guilty now for not listening properly. Thankfully it passed.

There was a bee today on my windowsill. *At this time of year!* I managed to get a teaspoon of sugary water near to it and it seemed to drink some and then it flew off. That made me feel happy for a moment or two and it made me think about the robin. Maybe the robin is keeping out of the way for a bit. Very sensible. It also made me think about how nature is the perfect, evolved system and how we have just messed it up by trying to intervene, or control, or make it better for just us. The system worked perfectly well, in total balance, and refines itself when it needs to. It will perhaps get rid of us and move on. It should.

Friday 6th February

I was called into a 'focus group' today at work so that we could discuss how the redundancy process has gone. We were there to assess if the process of sacking my colleagues had been handled well. We sat in a room whilst those being 'let go' continued at their desks and this appeared perfectly normal to those in charge here. They brought in some external consultants to assess our feedback and the process. Give me strength. They could have just called it 'conscience cleansing' rather than a focus group. I asked two questions. Could we keep some more staff instead of employing these consultants? (I pointed at them as I asked), and, are we having this session to ensure the next redundancy process will go more smoothly? And so, quite rightly, I was asked to leave the group early, which was great as I was dying for a wee following the complimentary beverages. It was all a mask as inside I was screaming *'Keep her, don't sack her for no reason, she is beautiful'*.

She looked over at me quizzically as I was clearly leaving early. I smiled as if I knew something or had done something clever. She may have misjudged my attempt as her face seemed to have faint hope of a reversal. I could not give her what she wanted. But I could give her so much more.

Saturday 7th February

Still no word from my sister.

I felt a hint of spring in the air and felt like I wanted to go to the garden centre. So, without thinking about it, I text her to see if she wanted to join me. I did this so quickly, that it wasn't that brave. If I had dwelled, I would have stopped myself or messed up the text. She replied 'Yes, sure, I'll meet you there, thank you! x' and everything, for a moment, felt amazing.

On the way there I fantasised about ending Mum's life. I thought it would be easy just to put a pillow across her face. I wouldn't take long. She is weak. And the struggle would be light. Perhaps, deep down, she would be grateful and see the mercy within the act. She would die thanking me inside, she would understand. I did some research into it at work as I had the chance to use someone else's computer. It would very much be an act of kindness. Best for everyone in the long run. There's a best way to do it to reduce the suffering.

Sunday 8th February

What a wonderful Saturday. We laughed, we looked at plants, we had coffee and cake. It was as carefree as my life could ever be. I got so carried away, I invited her round to help me sort the garden and to plant the new plants and I think she said yes. I was so caught up in the moment, I forgot to be me. So, I've no idea what is next, but it was all so lovely, so natural. Do I follow up or is that too much? Do I wait for her? I'll try not to think too much about 'next', I'll try to just enjoy the moment for a while.

In the late afternoon, I had an impromptu nap which was so rudely and abruptly ended by the phone ringing. A noise, which I feel, is now more and more uncommon. It was my sister. She talked me painstakingly through every detail of her illness and the needed procedure and it would seem she is only at the beginning of her journey. Is it wrong that I didn't care all that much? Maybe it was because I had just woken up. As soon as she rang and we started speaking the concern that had grown about her within me just, evaporated. It is not as if we are close. How come now I am involved? I'm not involved when anything goes well for her. I know very little of her. I know dates, I know things but I have no idea how she feels, what it is she is all about. Towards the end of the call the true purpose of the conversation revealed itself. I believe she wants me to pay for her to go private. Whilst neither of us actually knows the others financial situation the assumption is always that I have much more money than her. I was non-committal. I mean, why should I have to pay for that?

Monday 9th February

Apparently, we were seen together at the garden centre and so we are one of the office conversations today. We are the fuel of the office gossipers. This had better not affect things. Does she even know we are in the gossip? No one has approached me directly of course, which is good as I might just blush and make it worse. I've had a few of those looks from people as they pass my desk. I either ignore or look mildly confused.

I was brave enough to send a text from the train to see how she was, but I didn't get any reply so now I am worried, but dare not send another text as that might make me look a bit needy, a bit desperate or even weird.

Tuesday 10th February

A text on the way to work gave me all the joy imaginable as she asked me if we could go for a walk at lunchtime, but then I worried she wanted to talk about the gossip and maybe end our relationship. So, I was both excited and scared in equal measure, which meant I did very little work as I just watched the clock slowly tease me about how far away lunchtime was. I was wrong on both counts. She wanted to tell me that her ex-boyfriend has been in touch and what do I think she should do. How could I convey that she should never talk to him again, delete his number and erase him from her life without sounding like I was acting purely from self-interest. It was so hard but so right to tell her to look into her heart and imagine what the two scenarios might be like. I used the old trick of tossing an imaginary coin and then whilst it spins in the air, asking yourself which side you are hoping it will come down on. She was quiet for a little while and then looked deep into my eyes in a way that made my insides melt and my legs weak and she said that I was wise and caring and that she was glad we were friends.

I didn't get much done in the afternoon either and I was so distracted on the journey home I forgot to go to the shop and that left me with not many options for dinner, but I wasn't hungry. Well, not in that way.

Wednesday 11th February

On the way into work, I remembered that it is Valentine's day on Saturday. This is not something I've needed to really think about too much for a while, for years really, but this year it has left me with something of a quandary. Do I do something, do I buy a card for her? I decided to send her a text that said how I understood how it might be difficult for her this year and so if she wanted to meet up for a coffee or something I'd be really delighted to. Excellent move I thought. Emphasis off me and avoid the embarrassment of choice through my concern for her feelings. I felt like I got the words wrong in my message so I will see what happens next. I can't really buy a card or make any grand gesture, as that just feels wrong, and always corny, but if I could open up to her fully, I'd tell her that I love her beyond words and that I want her to be mine. That feeling did not pass all day.

Thursday 12th February

She text me back today, nearly 24 hours after I had text her. She said 'That's ok, thank you x' and I spent most of the day trying to analyse those four words and kiss.

Friday 13th February

How can anyone truly believe in superstition? I mean, who or what is it that they think is going to impact their day just because it is the 13th on a Friday? They magnify every turn of events and blame 'fate'. It's a warped sense of people wanting to believe there is a higher purpose, or some sort of God. All the different Gods were created by human brains and human imagination, so if there is something, it's probably beyond the capability of our intelligence to understand it. And if there is something, I trust they have better things to do than to play tricks on people because it is Friday the 13th.

Saturday 14th February

It is Valentines Day. I wouldn't have even thought about that being a thing if it wasn't for her and now, I cannot even text her. I looked at her reply again and eventually deleted the whole conversation. She has put me in something of a bad mood and even a long walk in the cold couldn't shake it. The robin reappeared but I felt like it was just there to tease me and that it was laughing at me, so I clapped my hands to shoo it away.

To pile it on, my sister text me to see how I was. I wanted to tell her that she cannot have any money, and so I just ignored it.

I ended up clearing out the cupboards and was very pleased that I only needed to throw out one tin of soup due to it being out of date. I run a tight ship.

Sunday 15th February

I thought about planning a summer trip to Cornwall today, so I looked online and found some nice looking accommodation but after a while the urge passed and I didn't bother. I feel somewhat unsettled and I don't like it. It's her. I'm suspended in time somehow.

A salesman knocked on my door today. I didn't realise that still happened. And on a Sunday. He was from the local hospice, or so he said. He said I should give him all my details and commit to a monthly direct debit. I mean, as if you would do that after some random stranger knocks on your door. He seemed very happy with himself and even after I politely said 'no' he still wished me a very nice day. I reckon it was a scam. If it wasn't, he is up against it around here. Later on I considered that he was indeed working on behalf of the hospice and it's ever needy residents so I felt bad. I went online and made a donation to them to help and also, in some way, to reward his efforts on a cold Sunday.

Monday 16th February

We all got an email today about an Easter ball. A morale boosting event apparently. The idiots couldn't even see the insensitivity of sending this out before the leavers had actually left. It turns out that if you are a 'leaver' you didn't get an invite. How horrible and thoughtless. It will have been the consultant's idea. Anyway, how can we even be thinking about Easter as Christmas is only just behind us. The commercial hamster wheel gets faster and faster and we spend more and more and get further and further away from knowing what really makes us happy. All of our warped calendar traditions have been turned into something even more warped to make rich people even richer.

I did wonder, on the train home, if I am capable of loving someone else, given that I don't really love myself. But I want her to be mine. Maybe we could go to Cornwall together. Is that too much?

Tuesday 17th February

I accidentally listened in to a conversation on the train this morning. One person consoling his friend for some reason or other. Giving him false encouragement about how good he is and that all he needs to do is believe in himself more. We really do lie to each other constantly. We do it to ease our way through situations, to make life easier on us, to make people feel better but does it really achieve that? How about a year of total honesty? Not harshness, or nastiness, just everyone being brutally honest with each other. I think the world would be a better place. There is no such thing as a 'white lie'. Advertisers and marketeers lie to you every day. Newspapers lie to you every day. Your family and friends lie to you every day. It's subtle, but it is still lies and although now impossible, the world would be a better place without lies.

Wednesday 18th February

Her redundancy got rubber stamped today. There is no way back now, not that there ever was. It made me feel more urgent about getting closer to her. Could I ask her round? Is it too early to arrange some gardening? What would she think of my house? Could I go round to hers? We had a nice chat and arranged to go for a coffee after work tomorrow. Another coffee in 'our' coffee shop. How to make her all mine? I need to open up to her a bit more I think, but it's not easy. Not for me anyway. And now I have the added complication of her maybe wondering if I just want to get at her redundancy money. Nothing could be further from the truth.

Thursday 19th February

Today was nothing but my time with her. We chatted more deeply than we have before. I spoke more too. I spoke of Cornwall, of being on my own and being single. Of the simple things in life. She spoke of finances, of her recent break up and being at a crossroads in her life. It sounded a bit corny to be honest. She looked amazing though. Her hair is so amazingly wonderful and her complexion and her skin are just perfection. Her eyes are the work of the devil, but her temperament is the work of angels. When we are connected and she looks at me, there is nothing else in the world, everything stops or is at least paused. I think I did quite well, but I felt things were just left hanging when I wanted a bit more, something more concrete for next. What do I do now?

I am not going to the Easter ball. I wonder if anyone will?

Friday 20th February

A text from my sister early in the morning didn't help my mood. *I know your game.* I have fully decided she doesn't not have any right to my money. I would never ask her. *Use your own money.* I didn't save up all these years for this. She'll have to wait or pay for it herself. That is fair enough. I didn't reply. Anyway, I have bigger things to think about.

I feel tired this week and in need of some rest.

Saturday 21st February

For some strange reason I sat and watched my wedding video today. I really need to get it converted from a video tape, or maybe it is time to just put it in the bin and move on. Everything is recorded nowadays, but this was filmed in a time when that was a special thing and so people look at the camera and pull faces or are at least aware something unusual is happening. That, in itself, brings a certain, long passed innocence. She looked way too good for me. The attention is all on her. I can see people thinking 'She's too good for him', it's written all over their faces. I look awkward and my hair looks really old fashioned. I am very thin and pale but not interesting. My suit looks a bit too big. My smile never reaches my eyes. I look uncomfortable and camera shy. It really is shame how it all turned out. It is for the best though. I felt some shame, maybe guilt, maybe regret, but it passed. Mainly, I just couldn't wait for it to finish.

Sunday 22nd February

I got a message today from an old friend. An old friend both in that he is old and that he, in my view, is really a former friend. I suspiciously await the revelation of what he really wants. He says he wants a 'drink'. I do miss wine a bit sometimes, so maybe I will.

I played some vinyl records today. Such a joy to place the needle on the outer groove and hear the faint crackle of anticipation. I also like how nobody knows I'm listening to it. There is no digital footprint or data being gathered about what to sell to me next. It's just me and the record player. As far as I know. It seems that young people are again onto this now as I understand vinyl is once again popular. All my records are old, or, as I prefer it, originals, but now maybe I have the chance to buy some new vinyl. I'd probably just buy the same records again as I can't really find any new music that I like.

Monday 23rd February

The journey into work was all about the anticipation of seeing her but also the realisation I am counting down the days of how many more times this will happen. For some strange reason, I thought about my mother and my sister too today.

We caught each other's eye across the office and when we saw each other, it was so familiar, almost like we have our own secret and I loved it. I feel so much braver now, it is so much easier. I just blurted out that we should meet this week and she just blurted out yes. We have started to lunch together almost every day. Just naturally. It's all so lovely. *Is she starting to become mine? Dare I dream?*

Tuesday 24th February

It'll soon be the anniversary. Four years. I think I'll always mark it but just by thinking about it and contemplating rather than by any of the other nonsense that has become the norm. Am I grateful for the extra time I've had, or do I wish I'd finished the job? I'm never going to know the answer to that. Not until it's too late anyway.

Wednesday 25th February

Work really seems to have changed. There seems to be an increased mismatch in the drive for profit and the pretence that we, the people, really matter to them. They've now employed a 'rewards manager' at the recommendation of the consultants, and it turns out he is the best friend of one of the consultants. You couldn't make it up. *Give me your watch and I'll tell you the time.* Jobs for the boys.

We now also have to put stickers up now to show how we are feeling and whether we want to chat. I put the same sticker up every day. I'm consistent. It's the one that basically says 'stay away from me'. It's the red one. I'd invent a fourth sticker if I could, to make sure people got the message. A deep crimson face of rage. Surely if our culture is right, and we know each other, we would just naturally know when to support or leave alone. It feels like we have gone back to primary school. We also have to work more flexibly and smarter and we have to trust each other more, apparently. Yes, I'm delighted to trust the management that just sacked half the staff. They truly do not even see the absurdity. But, of course, mainly we have to increase the company profits. It's all a bit like a mental health advert on Twitter, at best ironic and, at worst, insulting.

Thursday 26th February

My old friend James continues to pester. I'm still not sure what he wants but he clearly wants something otherwise he wouldn't have got in touch just out of the blue. I delayed responding but this doesn't seem to dishearten him, in fact, it only seems to encourage him. He asked for my address, the audacity. Truth is it hasn't changed but he is assuming it must have after all this time. What does he want? Neutral territory to begin with is safest. Why is he back in touch and why now?

Words, when used well, can be so beautiful yet most people have no idea how to use them properly.

Friday 27th February

We went for a coffee after work last evening and she was just so beautiful. I can happily write that I am in love with her. These feelings seem new to me though that must be a trick of the memory as I have been in love before. Or maybe, each time we are truly in love, the feelings are unique to the person we love. If that is the case, we should fall in love as many times as we can throughout our lives. But then, I suppose, there would be more endings, more heartbreak.

I just love to listen, I never interrupt. She smiles a small, ever so slightly crooked smile when she has said something witty or silly and each time it happens, I fall further. We have become really close, and I hardly know how it happened. I am so reserved about taking any steps to further this as it is as precious to me as cutting the world's largest diamond and I don't want to make a mistake that could prove fatal, that would shatter everything. *One false move.* At the same time though, I am aching to kiss her, to hold her and for our lives to become more entwined to a point of total inseparability.

Saturday 28th February

I kept busy today by cleaning, walking and generally making my house look brighter. I could do with some new décor and stuff, but I never have the inclination nor the skill to do it well, so I always just let that feeling pass. I decided to text her late afternoon and she replied almost immediately, which I loved. We are to meet for a walk tomorrow and my heart is full of joy.

James text me yet again in the evening but I dared to ignore it. Go away.

Sunday 29th February

The walk was bliss and without thinking I invited her round afterwards. I seemed to waffle on about my décor and the garden and all sorts of other rubbish, but she just laughed and said she would love to come round. I think something is happening. We seemed to stare at each other for a bit longer than is normal and we both just smiled. I also told her about the curse of the leap year and how, whenever there is a 29th February, I am cursed with bad luck. I even gave her the last four examples which are quite severe. She brushed this off, even giggled at the suggestion and in an instant and with a flick of her hair suggested this time it might well be the opposite. I could burst.

Monday 1st March

The world feels in step when the first of a month is a Monday. I dreamt of winning the premium bonds one million pound jackpot this morning on the bus. A daydream technically I suppose but it almost felt like I was asleep. I feel more tired in the mornings as I get older. I do always allow and enjoy that daydream just once a month. It feels good for my brain to indulge. It would seem already that the reality is reserved for at least one further month. I'll probably win £25 or nothing.

I never play the ghastly lottery though. In my view, premium bonds are an investment, but the lottery is just a tax on hope. Sometimes when I go for a walk, I see the same man scratching away at his seemingly daily scratch card and if I time it just right, or just wrong, I see the daily heartbreak he suffers permeate through his ageing and deeply wrinkled face.

Tuesday 2nd March

We had a 'gratitude session' at work today. Again, the hierarchy seem oblivious to the notion that half the staff are leaving at the end of the month, through no choice of their own, and that they are still here at the moment. Why on earth is this company so insensitive to this? The reward manager is asking people who have been forced to leave whether they would prefer a new coffee machine or a table tennis table. When he introduced himself to me properly and told me his role, I sarcastically asked him what he is going to do in the afternoons. The best bit was that my love heard it and she thought it was really funny. She did that laugh where you find it funny but you try to supress but can't fully. When she does it, and at my quip, it makes me the happiest man in the world and I feel so funny and clever. To be the cause of her amusement and to see her try to suppress her momentary joy is a natural wonder. The look of mischief she gave me could have moved a mountain or melted a glacier in an instant. Her eyes were given to her by the devil himself but she is pure of soul.

How have we got to needing 'gratitude sessions'? Can't everyone, or at least, very nearly everyone, see that we really have it all. We have it all. *Just look.*

I wonder if we are slowly replacing religion with this sort of thing.

Wednesday 3rd March

I've been told I have to book some holidays as I have some still left over from last year plus this year's allowance as well. I don't need any time off but maybe I could take some time in early April as she will be free after the 31st March. I'll ask her, if I dare. *I daren't.*

I spoke to my former mother this evening. Yes former. I hereby disown her. She casually let me know that she has taken to using her maiden name again now. And so, she is no longer Mrs O'Brien. It's like she wants to sever all ties, to remove all history. She also told me she has changed her will, but she wouldn't say what it was originally or what it now is, so that means nothing to me. She did make it sound like she had carried out a threat though and I felt like I will be getting less. That's why she mentioned it, out of spite and to cause something.

Why on earth would she do that? Change her name? Or change it back to be more accurate. There must be a reason. How can she be so casual about it? Why tell me she has changed her will when I had no idea what was in it anyway. I think I shall no longer address her as Mum. I will now call her Ms Hinchcliffe, if she is so intent on everyone else knowing her as that. We all have choices Ms Hinchcliffe. I thought about my Dad.

Thursday 4th March

Imagine yourself, without your brain and without your body. But still you, just you. What is that part of you that isn't your brain or your bodily organs. Sometimes I wonder and maybe hope that this is what might remain after physical death and sometimes I just long for the abyss we didn't know, the one before birth, to return. The nothingness. Just what are we if we are not our body or our brain? How will I find out for sure, or indeed will I, ever?

Friday 5th March

I spoke to James at lunchtime. I needed to get it out of the way. Isn't it funny how some people in life somehow force you to play a character for them? I fell straight back into that person, and I'd forgotten he existed, but as soon as we started talking there he was. As soon as we hung up, I came back to me and had lunch with my love. I hate him for somehow forcing me to play a character I'd rather not be, just for him. How many other such characters do I have hidden away?

Saturday 6th March

I went for a walk so early today just so I could hear only my footsteps and the birdsong and nothing else. Just my tiny little impression on the world and all of the splendid sounds nature provides. I thought about everyone's desire nowadays to *get attention* and how we all seem to have forgotten to *pay attention*. Nature teaches us but we seem to refuse the lesson. There was more than a hint of spring nudging its way in and an inevitability about winters imminent departure. Nature always wins. Always. Sometimes she takes her time, is ever so gradual and slow but she always prevails. Evil is much quicker.

Sunday 7th March

I am never getting married again as it is just an illusion of permanence. It's a religion based societal norm. It means nothing to the logical and everything to the mentally ill. Its days are numbered and thank goodness for that. It is a legal obligation and there aren't even any tax advantages anymore.

But what if *she* asked me?

Monday 8th March

There really is no time like the present. We went for lunch today and from nowhere I invited her round at the weekend. She said yes so naturally I barely flinched. It was only on the journey home that I realised how brave I had been, what a big step I had taken. I am on some sort of roll, I think.

Tuesday 9th March

I wasn't myself today.

It is close to the first of two anniversaries today. I'd sooner forget the first but it did lead to a chain of events upon its second anniversary. The 9th March is forever, sadly, carved into my brain and I cannot remove its stain. I decided not to deal with this fully today, or any other day. I will not allow my brain to win, but in some ways it did. In some ways it always does.

Wednesday 10th March

More texts from James. I wish he would go away but he simply won't and so I will need to see him once to kill him off for good. I suggested we go to the local pub, and he said he hadn't been there for years and he couldn't believe it was still my local. I haven't actually been in there for about fifteen years, but it's still the nearest one to me because I haven't moved. Why do people want to move house so much? It will be awful and no doubt awkward, but I will go, make an excuse early and then it's done. Something still nags me about what he wants. People always want something from you and I remember him as a bit of a chancer.

Thursday 11th March

Be kind to the machines so that one day, when we are surplus to them, they might be kind to us.

Friday 12th March

I cleaned the house from top to bottom in the evening as she will see it, see me, tomorrow. I even changed some of the pictures on the wall. I paid particular attention to the toilets as she might need to use them. I threw out things I probably didn't need to and then I went to the shop to ensure there is nothing she can ask for that I don't have. I don't know enough about her to have covered all bases but I think I can look just about sophisticated enough with what I bought. I also bought a sexier sounding deodorant even though I had no idea how it smells. I'm very tired now but me and my house are ready. One day she might live here. That's the thought I went to sleep on.

Saturday 13th March

The day started so beautifully, why did something or should I say, someone have to spoil it. I went for a lovely walk and then we met for a coffee and some light breakfast. We walked back to mine, and I was so nervous to show her my home. I'd forgotten about nerves and how they affect you. She walked in and barely looked at the place. She said it was nice. She asked why there are no pictures of my wife on show which I thought was a bit odd. I explained that I've been through all the stages of grief and that I need to move on with my life. *She's dead, not me!*

I wanted to kiss her so much and I even dared to think of going up to bed with her but instead I acted like a nervous teenager seemingly trying to impress her by showing her my garden and favourite possessions. I spoke too quickly and not quite in my normal voice and I flitted and fidgeted to the point where I didn't even like myself. In fact, I hated myself a bit at that moment but then she came over and took my hand into hers. I find it hard to be just me. I have to find my character in any given situation. She explained how she had become *'fond'* of me. My heart was racing, and I was dry-mouthed and speechless but no matter as she just kept talking, giving me more. It sounded semi-rehearsed, which I loved. She seemed to be saying let's move forwards, *let's be more.* I was in dreamland and had no response. I simply said yes and then yes again, like an obedient schoolboy. I think I had a tear in my eye which I tried to supress and then the blasted doorbell went. How dare anyone or anything intrude so rudely and at this wonderful moment. Who on earth could it be? The chime instantly broke our beautiful spell and it couldn't be restored. I headed to the door with some fury and ready to engage with this intruder, this thief. I couldn't wait to get rid of them. It could only be a stranger, I hadn't ordered anything and nobody was due at my door. It was James, of all people. I'd forgotten how brash he was, how arrogant and he invited himself in. I wanted to kill him on the spot. He wandered in and said that the place hadn't changed much. He entered the kitchen and looked in my fridge as if both looking for refreshment and at the same time judging me. As he walked into the lounge *with his shoes still on,* he saw her and made the most chauvinistic and childish noise I have ever heard, followed with what can only be defined as a misogynistic hello. The worse thing of all is that they seemed to be getting on quite well. I became some kind of gooseberry, some kind of server or staff member in my own home, and I had allowed it to happen. I couldn't stop it. I can't play two characters at once. She laughed at his jokes and his anecdotes. He has such confidence. Call me Jimmy he said. Since when? Neither of them were talking to me. I provided drinks and snacks and my rage began to grow. As I entered the room with their latest request for drinks *they were swapping telephone numbers.* Was she looking at him with affection? *Did she want him?*

I tried again but I just couldn't play both these parts at once. I felt the turmoil, like an actor trying to be in two films at once. It's impossible.

Finally, I pooled enough rage into courage to move him on and out of the house. I made up some excuse that we were due out so he would have to go. He tried to tag along but I had just enough craft to prevent that from happening. *I had predicted that move, Jimmy.* He left. I still have no idea what he wants from me. He was too distracted by her. That means I will have to see him yet again. I turned back into the room, hardly able to ignore the mess he had brought in underfoot, when she said 'thank god' he had gone I was so relieved. I deleted his number from her phone when she went to the toilet. She'll think she hadn't saved it properly, hopefully. The job is only half done though as he could still message her. *I need to intercept him before he thinks to do that.* When she came back into the room I was hoovering. She laughed at me. She could probably see my dissolving rage. I couldn't stop myself from cleaning up his mess and at the same time trying to remove all trace of him from my house. It was a physical and a psychological act. But her laughter brought me back into character and I switched the hoover off and everything seemed fine again in an instant.

She left soon after as she had to go but we did have just enough time for a chat and a kiss on the cheek. I told her I am deeply fond of her too and she smiled and blushed. That made me blush too which is another thing I hadn't done in such a long time. Blushing and nervousness make me feel like a teenager.

She never mentioned my new deodorant, which, on reflection, I think is probably a good thing. I hope she liked it. I'm not sure I do.

All my mistakes are in the past, so I do not need to live with guilt. You'll never be able to link me to anything I've done anyway. I live with a clear conscience, but today taught me that jealously is another thing all together.

Sunday March 14th

James text me to say thanks for inviting himself into my house and nearly ruining my day. He has the bare faced audacity to ask if we were a couple. I told him not to text her as after he had left, I told him she said he was a 'complete wanker'. That felt good. He didn't reply. I hope that's him gone now. It had better be, for his sake. He is like a bad penny though.

Monday March 15th

It is the anniversary today but not a day I can mark. This is the anniversary day in my eyes, if not the eyes of the official, outside world. The only day I can outwardly show my false respects is the anniversary of the funeral. Anyway, there is literally nobody who notices now. I won't even get a card, everyone has moved on. I did look out for the robin to try and somehow connect some sentimental dots, but it's probably dead.

I felt a strange desire and impulse, or maybe obligation, to ring Ms Hinchcliffe, but it soon passed.

Tuesday March 16th

The rain abated today so we had the chance to go for a walk at lunchtime. I brought James up in an attempt to end that for good but I didn't want to directly ask if he had text her in case this alerted her to somehow look at her phone for his number. She seemed to have forgotten all about him, so I quickly moved on. I talked about her leaving work and then dared to ask if I should book a few days off in early April so we could have some time together. What makes me so brave at lunchtimes? I think it is to do with not taking any time to think. She beamed back the best 'yes' I have ever received and everything felt perfect. She instinctively raised both arms and I felt a compulsion to turn that into a hug but I didn't quite dare so it was all a bit uncomfortable. We seemed to hold our gaze at that moment for about an hour, but it was probably about two seconds. I put the holiday request in at work as soon as I got back and I just daydreamed the afternoon away about being away with her for a spell. What is happening here and please let it continue.

Wednesday 17th March

My holiday request was declined as we will be 'short of staff at this time'. Yes, that's because you've made people we need redundant! *You told me to book some!* I complained and a compromise was reached so I have the second week in April off. What dare I suggest we do? I want to go away with her. Somewhere, *anywhere, I don't care, I don't care.* The same bed. How dare I write that. I certainly dare not suggest that, but I was saved by the incessant rain today as it meant I had no way to properly talk to her and face it.

There was the suggestion of after works drinks to celebrate St Patricks Day. Apparently, there would be a great atmosphere, a 'buzz' no less, in town. I asked if anyone was Irish or indeed remotely so and was accused of being a party pooper. Nobody was though, and nobody seemed to know much anything about St Patrick himself. Not even his surname. Are there any new saints?

Thursday 18th March

I text her this morning from the bus to tell her my holidays have been approved and 'what shall we do?' Maybe she will realise that I must have known this yesterday and wonder why I waited until the morning to tell her. I hope she doesn't think I am being overly relaxed about our mini break. I also realise I have given her the question, the problem of 'where and what' to answer, which is me being a coward but hopefully she will see this as chivalrous and unassumptive. I just don't want to mess this up or even put a foot wrong.

Friday 19th March

Thank goodness it is Friday. I am coming to hate this place more and more and I am questioning why I need it in my life. The 'redundants' as they are now known collectively, or the 'R's' even (I think it's pronounced 'arse'), are still around and most of them are like a bad smell. But it's not their fault and the more you consider it, the more you realise they just got rid of the higher earners. I was lucky to survive, or maybe unlucky. So, we will be shorthanded and inexperienced come April and in the meantime, we have a population of people who have no other interest than to disrupt and gossip until they leave. Well done everyone.

Saturday 20th March

My sister text me today to ask me for £18,000. Just like that. *In a text*. Either I give her the money or she has to wait around 5 months for her 'procedure'. I felt mainly anger, like she has somehow put her life in my hands. If only I had such a privilege, I could sort everything. I think it was Buddha who said, 'If I choose not to accept the gift, then to whom does it belong'. Wise words. This is a 'gift' I certainly do not wish to 'accept'. How can anyone reply to a text like that? She says she knows 'it's a lot' and has asked me to think about it and let her know by Wednesday. I can let her know now but cannot believe I am being forced to say such a thing, and by text message.

It nibbled away at my insides all day and it grew in my stomach bit by bit until I let out a huge roar in the garden. I don't know if anybody heard. I like to think I would never put anyone in that situation.

Sunday 21st March

I thought about asking my love what to do about my sister. But as I had already decided I realised just how bad it might make me look in her eyes. If *she* needed my heart, she could have it. I would *die* for her but I'm not sure I'd even go to the end of the road for my sponging, needy, part-time sister. Blood relatives, I ask you. She is never in contact unless she wants something and the way she has gone about this business is both distasteful and controlling. But I will seize back the control in my reply.

Blood relatives expect without putting in any effort. True friends put in the effort and expect nothing.

Monday 22nd March

I replied to my sister last thing last night. I said I could not help and that it was unfair to ask. A text deserves only a text back. She replied almost immediately saying it could be life and death and she had nowhere else to turn. That did pinch a little and pull on the family heart strings but why on earth should I give her £18,000? So, I replied with a 'sorry'. Just one word. Sorry. And then silence. I slept well. No one has given me anything. No one has ever given me anything. There's so many assumptions and arrogance in her request. I'm trying to not let it annoy me too much but it certainly won't bring us any closer.

Tuesday 23rd March

My princess has suggested a little cottage she knows in Devon and my heart is dancing with joy. I hope she hasn't been there with another though, as that wouldn't be right. It had better be clean.

It will soon be Easter and so the religious types were out in force today. We had a visit, at work, from some local group or other. I think the consultants thought it would be spiritual for us to discuss such matters in a 'group setting'. It was a miscalculation as it just ended up being a debate about blind faith. I enjoyed it and even contributed once. I explained the maths of the situation, so they just moved on. Whether the whole thing is true or not, how did we get to chocolate eggs? You couldn't make it up, but literally somebody did! Whatever it is, you can't call it a fad, they've been peddling this for over two thousand years. I doubt the ideas of these consultants will last that long so some credit must be due, just for the longevity of all of this.

Wednesday 24th March

Another demonstration again today outside another nearby office and so I took an interest and had a chat to one of the calmer ones. It is an ethical protest about cruelty to animals which the company they were targeting is apparently violating. They are not breaking any laws, but this group are asserting, with some force it must be said, that what the company is doing is wrong. I explained to the lady I spoke to that laws were made to follow morals and not the other way round. Our morals guide us as humans and then laws are made to allow us to have legal guidelines to follow those morals. Well, that was the original idea before politicians realised their power created such lucrative personal opportunity. She seemed somewhat energised by this and asked me if I would join the group. I would have quite liked to as I agreed with what she had to say but I explained I couldn't be late for work. She said, to watch or to do, it's up to you, which I found both poetic and appealing. We exchanged a lovely smile and I felt better about my fellow humans. I really liked her.

Later at lunch I wondered how did we get so arrogant as to believe animals are there for our use and that we are somehow above them, separate, better in some way? We are one and we are in this together. I bet most of the staff who work in that company have dogs. We are nothing if not a duplicitous race.

Thursday 25th March

She is in the final week of working here and I felt angry again today. Only five days left including this one. Why would I want to stay here? She will not be here, the pressure is increasing and there will be less of us. I wish I had been offered a pay out now. A big pay out at that. Is that chance now gone forever? She seems really calm about it. She keeps thanking me for my support. I wish she would move on to thanking me for my love.

She doesn't seem to walk, she seems to just glide along. I love to watch her.

Friday 26th March

Everyone seems to ignore the most fundamental of human problems. There are just too many of us. It is never discussed as far as I can see. On the train this morning I imagined a world where cancer was contagious. I shivered at the thought. Imagine our inability to cope with that. Imagine the behaviours it would trigger from different groups of people. There would be those that would look after just themselves. They would retreat and wish to buy a gun to shoot anyone who came close. They would save their own skin above all else. These people are easy to spot in day-to-day life. They have numerous locks on their front door, big gates and numbers on their bins. They are in it for themselves and protect ideals and territory with equal amounts of ferocity. They live in the belief that they have something they need to hang onto. Then there would be those looking to solve the humanitarian crisis. Those that give themselves to a greater cause. Those that have compassion. They see and act on the bigger picture, and for each other. They are also instantly recognisable too. One thing is for sure, it would be an indiscriminate way of there being less of us, albeit a terribly cruel and painful way. There is no other way left now than through a natural accident or cycle. Let nature slowly resolve, and she no doubt will. If left to humans to decide who remains, they would self-select the richest people. It's a huge mistake to think the richest people are the best people. They are simply the ones with money. Many inherited it and so have done nothing, many gained money with a cutthroat attitude to business. That's one skill but having money gives an overrated position in our society. Those with money will do anything to hang onto it. All the best people throughout history, all of them, are not remembered for their wealth. I am sure nature will sort this out for us in her own time.

The train seemed to stop sharply, which is quite unusual. This broke my spell and brought me right back to the moment, to where I truly was and with a bump.

Saturday 27th March

Deathly silence from my sister. It would seem I am pushed out from her inner circle now that I have stated I am unwilling to stump up thousands of pounds for her. She didn't speak to me before so it would seem she only wanted to talk to me to gain the money. I think this vindicates my decision and absolves me of any need to dwell. I don't wish her any harm and do slightly resent the position she has put me in. Some people are very good at that, and she is one of them.

Sunday 28th March

The clocks changed overnight and every year there are less and less clocks to change as a computer somewhere, somehow, now changes them for you. In they creep, bit by bit, by stealth or through the sale of a lie. Your every move is being tracked and you pay a monthly subscription for the privilege.

Who benefits from this changing of the clocks anyway? Surely it just means everyone has their schedule thrown out by an hour. They sell it as if it creates daylight which is preposterous. More non-sensical tradition, another one of many. These traditions offer a false comfort. Everything is temporary.

I went for a long walk today and connected with nature. Unfortunately, both the beginning and end of my walk meant I had to endure suburbia and I had the mispleasure of seeing a rather scruffy looking individual receiving a McDonalds from a man on a motorbike. She came to the door looking like stig of the dump. No self-care, or much self-respect in evidence as far as I could see then she pulled out two big bags of McDonalds and disappeared back into her untidy, badly lit hovel. I made a thousand assumptions on the spot and they were all bad. The whole thing felt somewhat anti-natural to me. Is this where we are? I shouldn't be so nosy and should just let people be.

We shared the most fantastic Sunday lunch together and then she came back to mine. All unplanned but the spontaneity was fabulous and didn't stop. She seemed a little restless when we got back and then she just grabbed me and kissed me and took me upstairs. She led the way and I followed and straight afterwards I fell asleep and I would have been quite happy never to have woken up again. I genuinely thought about asking her to live with me, but something stopped me. She told me she has never felt happier, and I replied without the need to think, that neither had I. I hate just agreeing and repeating in reply to anything, but it was one hundred percent true, and I think she knew that.

Monday 29th March

When I saw her at work today it felt like I was looking at the other half of me. We can't not smile when we make eye contact. It matters not that everyone sort of knows now. She leaves this place on Wednesday and I feel determined to follow and then we can both be free. *Together and free.*

I really felt like I was winning at life today. I know this is temporary, a thought that comforts me in bad times, but just let me enjoy this wonderful time. I literally want for nothing.

Tuesday 30th March

We must have sent each other one hundred texts just on the way in to work. I quite like texting as I have an extra moment to think before I send so I can be a touch more witty than in conversation. I have so much more to learn about her and I can't wait. Every discovery just adds another extra dimension to how I feel. It's like wandering around a beautiful castle with new rooms to find. Everything new about her just makes her more loveable. The setting is perfect and the opening of each door just shows you something more, something new, something extra, something delightful. I am in no rush to exhaust this journey. We must take our time and enjoy and revel in every next moment. She is perfect and she is mine, all mine.

Wednesday 31st March

Her last day at work. She was made a fuss of today and I had the luxury of standing back a little. I know she's mine now, so I don't need to compete with them for her attention on her last day. We are greater than office colleagues. *So much greater.* Seemingly she has a circle of friends. *A whole circle.* I was perturbed to see so much telephone number swapping. She shouldn't just give her number out due to the emotion of leaving the office. She should be leaving these people behind, not creating further ties. People just tossing their numbers at each other, it made my blood boil. I will look at her phone later to check it. My number is private and for the selected few. I hope she didn't read hers out so loudly that someone could just have it without her knowing.

She was given quite a good number of gifts and then fear stunned my back and tingled my spine as I heard one of her closer colleagues say that the gift was a joint leaving and birthday present. It seems her birthday is tomorrow. I had no idea. She didn't say. I have absolutely no idea how old she is. She must have had a lot of April fool jokes as a child. I have just a small number of hours. Not enough time for an online rescue plus there is literally no one I can ask for help. I've never been any good at presents. We don't need more stuff and presents are generally just 'more stuff'. What am I to do?

Thursday 1st April

It's her birthday and yet also her first day not here at work. A double celebration perhaps, but it didn't feel quite right. She didn't reply to my texts on the way in which I did not like. But maybe she is just staying in bed this morning. I text her to say 'Happy Birthday x x' but for some reason I typed it in Spanish. I think I was trying to look a touch sophisticated. I only know a little bit of Spanish anyway. Anyway, I later explained that I had only overheard that it was her birthday yesterday and so I would deliver her present when we go on our mini-break, just to buy myself a bit more time. I realise, with my plan, there is also an increased pressure, but I was in a bit of a corner. I ended up sending a stream of texts without reply and I wondered if my efforts had seemed a bit lame to her? I think she was enjoying my struggle just a little bit and I loved that.

At work we all received an email asking us not to participate in April Fools jokes as they are demeaning and 'in contravention of our health and safety policy'. All this did was alert some to the fact that they might like to try an April fools joke, a thought that otherwise would probably not have occurred to them. *Please keep off the grass.* Someone put salt in the sugar dispenser, apparently. *I do hope nobody died.*

Friday 2nd April

The two of us are going out for a meal tonight at her favourite restaurant. I hope she hasn't been there with anyone else, another man I mean. I hope she wants to come back to mine afterwards and stay the night. I love waking up and seeing her still asleep. She barely moves nor makes a sound and it is the most peaceful thing I have ever witnessed.

Saturday 3rd April

We dined, we came back, we spoke with such truth and openness and we went to bed. We just cuddled until she fell asleep and then, when I woke, she was still asleep, hardly making a noise at all until eventually I cuddled her awake. Her broken voice whispered 'I love you' and life can be perfect.

Later she went home so I just ached for her for the rest of the day. I want us to live together. *I think.* I did notice she had lots of messages and alerts on her phone as she left. Who is trying to get her attention? Who are all these people? She is mine and only mine.

James, or 'Jimmy' to his friends and fancies, text me again today. Please just go away. He says we should go out for a drink this week. I find it hard to reply. It only seems to encourage him, not dissuade him.

Sunday 4th April

It was the first anniversary of the funeral today and I didn't want to write that in black and white and I didn't want to mark it in anyway whatsoever. I thought nobody would remember. It seems some busybody at work had mentioned the date to my angel and so she felt the need to bring it up and she brought some flowers over and asked if I would like her to accompany me to the graveside. She just assumed I wanted to go. I said thanks for the flowers and that I would go later on, but I didn't. I just put the flowers in my neighbour's bin after dark and carried on with my day as normal. I was careful and made sure they did not just sit on the top. I have also noted that Ms Hinchcliffe and my sister both failed to send even a text about it. That's because there was nothing in it for them. My family, the parasites. They only appear when their mouths are empty.

Monday 5th April

It is the last day of the tax year. It will be ages until I get my P11d and am able to do my tax return. I could do it today if I had that. I am owed £238.81, or thereabouts.

Tuesday 6th April

A new tax year but no real change at work. Meetings about meetings about meetings about meetings about meetings. More strategies than action. More horseshit than the local farmer would know what to do with. Committees to oversee committees. More resets and break out areas than you could throw a stick at. I sat in one meeting today, overseen by a consultant of course, where I watched a man slowly die in front of me due to gaining absolutely no engagement from his audience whatsoever. This wasn't because people were trying to be mean, it was because people generally had no idea what he was talking about and so no one wants to stick their head up above the parapet for fear of looking as stupid as him. In years gone by, I would have helped him out a little, but honestly, why should I? I think Napoleon said, 'never interrupt your enemy when he is making a mistake' and that rang true a little today. I think I'll have to get serious about getting out of here. I'll re-read the terms of my share option again when I get home and then I'll look to plan my exit. Thinking about that and thinking about our impending trip away got me through until home time.

Wednesday 7th April

Death by data today. Do these people not see that at some point we have to do the actual work to provide the data for them to badly analyse. They miss the point because, to them, there isn't one, other than earning their ridiculous fees. And I have seen the invoices. Eyewatering stuff. There will be nothing left to measure soon. They love to tinker, to strategise, to formulate smart looking documents. I'm not sure these consultants have ever been at any coal face in their lives. One of them looks about twelve and he hides all his insecurities behind a veneer of arrogance. He came over to see me today and when I pointed something out, he looked perplexed. I said 'ask your Dad' and immediately I felt mean. I'd apologise if I cared.

My share option says that on the first of July the shares are mine and that's that. I shall resign on the 2nd, just to be on the safe side. That's not long at all.

Thursday 8th April

I haven't seen her since Sunday and so I became a little bit nervous about things on the bus this morning. I text her but it took me ages to get the words right and then I overthought it so ended up making a mess. She text straight back though to say she was excited and looking forward to the weekend and she put two kisses. So then I thought that everything might be okay. Am I supposed to do anything I haven't thought of? At least I have her birthday gifts now. I hope she likes them.

Friday 9th April

I am so excited today and therefore work was like surfing on a wave. I was in such a good mood. I even genuinely helped out one of the consultants with a question, which I immediately regretted. I later saw the young consultant in the kitchen, and so, without actually saying sorry I explained I knew I was mean to him the other day and that I didn't mean it. He didn't react. Not even a blink. Maybe he is as hard as nails after all. Whatever, I felt better for saying it. There's never any need to be mean or intentionally nasty to anyone.

Later on, I actually had to ask him something. It was only logistical but I didn't really want him to feel that I needed anything from him. Anyhow I asked him and jokingly he said 'Ask your Dad!' as if he had completed a joke and gained an upper hand, or maybe he was just trying to make friends. Later on, I thought it was quite a nasty thing to say. Anyway, quite obviously I said 'My Dad is dead' without a flicker of emotion. He just looked down and then I left. Thirty love to me, maybe thirty fifteen.

Saturday 10th April

It is the work 'Easter ball' today and I am glad I didn't go. I am sure this will be frowned upon and it could be argued that it might have been better to go and look the enemy right in the eye rather than avoid it. But life is too short and my personal investment at work has dwindled to next to nothing. Plus, it is not long until the maturity of my share option, so I can just leave then and be free. My main focus today was to pack for our first mini break. I somehow felt embarrassed to do it. I'd been putting it off. I feel like my possessions are somehow not quite good enough to accompany her. It's a strange feeling and I put it down to nerves. I wish I'd bought a new suitcase at least to make me look a bit more modern. Hopefully she won't mind or notice. They are all hard and shiny these days with wheels. I can't wait until we set off tomorrow. We've been texting each other all day and I probably won't sleep. I can't remember the last time I had to pack for anything. Not seeing her for a few days has made me want this, want her, all the more.

Sunday 11th April

She came over to pick me up and was bang on time, to the minute, which I loved. She looked so elegant and is a good driver. Very composed. She had made a playlist of songs she thought we might like but I hadn't heard of any of them, except for the very old ones. She likes The Eagles, *how cute is that*. James text me when we were travelling and when she asked me who it was, I just said 'no-one' which was perfectly true. When we stopped at the services it turned out that he had text her too which caused a mini stir as it revealed that she hadn't saved his number, which she found odd. He signed his text off with his name so there was no way around the issue. I said she mustn't have saved it properly and was hopefully convincing. She replied to him and saved his number which infuriated me almost as much as not knowing what they were saying. I couldn't show too much interest. I need to intervene here so will see James and work that out. I bet he was flirty with her. Is that really the first time he has text her since he invited himself into my house? Seems a little odd to me.

When we arrived at the cottage it could have not been more perfect. I didn't ask if she had been here with anyone else as I had totally stopped caring about any possible answer and just the question would have really lowered the mood. Idyllic isn't nearly enough to describe our setting. I flippantly suggested that we buy it and live there and in an instant it stopped sounding like the joke it was half meant to be. Shivers went down my back. *Really, maybe?*

You have to drive over a little bridge to get to the gravel drive and that makes you feel more beautifully isolated and separate from the world. The only eye stain is the hot tub which looks like it landed outside after being dropped uncaringly from a great height. The windows are all single pane and wooden and painted green. It's a cottage that rattles but that only gives it more charm. The door creaks and the internal doorways are low so you have to stoop. It is perfect. We drank wine and lit the fire after dinner. We laughed and I played with her hair. *Where did I get such confidence?* We went to the same bed so naturally. Even in my own diary, which is only for me, modesty prevents me from writing about and recording our intimacy. Intimacy has been forgotten. Sex has become a badge, a thing to do, a question of status and accomplishment and intimacy has been totally neglected. We reached the highest physical plane that two people can, we were as one, she was completely and totally mine as I was hers, just for that, all too short a time. No one else existed in the world. No words were needed as we communicated fully and explicitly. I don't think I've ever felt that open, that vulnerable, that loved or loving. I took, I gave, we shared, we were one being for that time. I wished these moments would never pass and that we could be frozen in time.

Monday 12th April

If ever a day didn't feel like a Monday, this was it. Could life be like this for us all of the time if I left work? I dare not bring this up out loud as the thought is so perfect, so idyllic that it could only be spoilt and soiled through talking. We walked and walked. We stopped for coffee and lunch. We walked, we sat, we chatted. I knew these were the best moments of my life as they were happening. This induced a strange mixture of total happiness and deafening sadness as I both enjoyed yet wanted to cling and prolong every passing second. We went back to the cottage, opened a bottle of wine and watched a film by the open fire. She fell asleep on me but when I realised, I just pulled the most content smile any man could pull. I could have stayed there for ever. I half carried her to bed and cuddled her into a deeper sleep. I didn't want to fall asleep myself, I just wanted to watch her but eventually the gods pulled my eyelids down and we slept together, alone as one.

Tuesday 13th April

Another day that can only be regarded as perfect. *Is this real life?* I kept thinking of the song 'Perfect Day', but I think someone once told me that was about how taking heroin feels. Still, I can't imagine anything feeling as good as this mini break feels, here with my darling. I gave her the birthday gifts I had bought for her today. I apologised for them being late. She said she loved them but it somehow didn't feel entirely authentic. They seemed quite paltry once she had opened them so I couldn't stop myself half apologising and then trying to move on quickly. I'll do better next year. Then she leapt towards me and kissed me and threw her arms around me and everything felt wonderful again.

Wednesday 14th April

It is the last full day and night of our holiday today and time cannot go slow enough, but the clock has no sympathy. Maybe time does sometimes speed up and slow down. How would we ever know? Being away, and our impending return made me think about my house. Is it okay? Will the post have been properly pushed through the letterbox? Will there be any parcels? I hope everything is alright. I hope the garden is okay. Maybe I have been burgled? I tried to stop worrying about it, but it hung around in my mind.

Thursday 15th April

We travelled back and still everything felt perfect. I thought I would feel sad but I didn't. When we stopped for coffee she asked me, so very gently, if I had imagined us living together. Without properly thinking I said of course I had. I perhaps sounded a little bit too keen. I didn't mean this as acceptance of an offer as I didn't feel like there had been an offer but then I worried I had pushed it all too far and I didn't want it to be irreversible, so I then asked about practicalities. I pushed twice in the wrong way and at the wrong point. I can be such a bumbling idiot at times. I replaced overzealous romance and possibility with practicality and risk. It made it seem further away. The truth is I am not sure. I still haven't seen her house yet and that will give me more, vital information about her.

Friday 16th April

It being Good Friday got the better of me and in a moment of weakness I text James, Jimmy, whatever, to see if he wanted a drink tonight. My sole focus was his phone and to eliminate him from our lives. He immediately replied 'yes' and so the time was set.

With no work and full rest, I would be at my most alert and inventive.

When I arrived at the pub he was already there. He had audaciously bought me a pint of bitter. *I mean, as if I would drink that.* I was polite in my correction and he said 'no matter' as he would just drink it himself. Possibly his plan all along. I ordered a lime and soda and could see the disappointment on his face. I'm not a real man, or at least a very boring one, as I don't drink copious amounts of booze. The cavemen are still living among us.

He was unusually nice once the silly act faded away. I saw a different James, possibly a lonely chap who survives with a brazen façade. I could have even felt a little sorry for him, but I had work to do. I watched him carefully scroll on his phone and easily learned his phone opening pin. People are so flagrant with this information, perhaps in the general belief no one is out to get them. Next, I had to separate him from his phone and this was remarkably easy too. He pushed it into his back pocket and so when he sat on the bar stool it was sticking out. I waited until he needed the loo and like some sort of professional pick pocket, I easily removed the phone from his pocket and quickly concealed it from his view. A member of the bar staff saw so when he had gone I joked with her that I was teaching him a lesson. She bought it, she laughed. But I had miscalculated badly and stupidly. He had the text conversation on his phone and so I could hardly delete that and then her number. It would look too obvious and as I pondered this, I saw the message exchange between them.

'Hiya gorgeous, Lovely to meet you. If you ever dump that loser and want a real man then give me a bell xxx'

'I hope you're joking'

'Half joking I suppose. You are way too gorgeous for him and we got on really well. I'd love to get to know you better xxx'

'I think it is better if you don't text me anymore. It was nice to meet you though'

'Not even a kiss on your replies? Xxx'

Days pass

'Sorry if I came over a bit strong, I just really liked you. It would be nice to stay in touch x'

Him again, the next day

'So you are not even talking to me now? X'

'I never really was'

'Suit yourself but it would be nice to see you again at some point. Let me know if you want to hook up xx'

No reply

I felt the fury of his assertions, the audacity, the cheek, the insults but I had to remain calm. At least my darling had responded well, but why respond at all, does she like him a bit, deep down? Was she enjoying the attention and the kisses? Was she simply playing hard to get and keeping an option open?

He arrived back from the toilet so I shut the phone down and waved it at him as if to say 'see what I have here'. He sat back down and said he was relieved to have it back even though he hadn't realised it had been missing. What a stupid thing to say. He probed a few times about my darling but I stonewalled him. No more fuel for your depraved and inappropriate texts from me. And then I stuck the knife in. As cool as a cucumber I said it was nice to see him but actually not that nice. We didn't seem to really have anything in common and so I told him I was leaving and didn't see any real reason to stay in touch. I actually said that, and he looked crestfallen. I really enjoyed his expression, the emotion in his face reacting to my cold, calm and clinical assertion. He was speechless as I said goodbye. It's more than he deserved. Goodbye indeed. Good riddance and whilst I couldn't delete her from his phone I have the upper hand, the knowledge of what he did.

Saturday 17th April

She came round early to help me look for some new stuff for my house. I thought that if she helped me choose, she would be more invested and maybe it would subconsciously make her feel more comfortable moving in at some point. I do think I want that. I keep getting a nagging feeling that I have never been to her house though, so I gently explored, but she softly avoided. Is there an issue?

It was lovely to look, to shop, with her. She makes the mundane, even the boring somehow irresistible. Plus, a second person gave me more confidence in my taste and although we like different things, I appreciated her view and liked what she eventually chose. She said it was exciting and that I had a lovely big house that she could help spruce up. It's not that big. *Does she live in a tiny space, I wonder?*

Her phone kept buzzing and it annoyed me that people were trying to invade our time. Why do we seem so unable to resist a buzzing phone? She then said that James had text her. I tried to look non-caring, but I asked her to share. She asked if he was a bit creepy and I said he had a terrible reputation with former girlfriends and that's why I didn't want to be close to him. I explained he had turned up out of the blue recently. I added in, for good measure, that he had asked me for money and that he had a drugs habit and a criminal record. I made it sound so plausible, like it was difficult to share but she had some sort of right to know. And I think it did the trick. But then she seemed angry at me for not telling her before. How could I? I had only just made it up. She asked me what to do. I told her to delete the messages, not to reply and then delete his number and, without hesitation, she dutifully did. She said I always know what to do and she smiled and kissed me as if to say we are together and I will protect her. I was too modest to agree but it all made me feel so strong, so useful and, even though I hate to admit it, it massaged my ego. Part of me wished others could have seen it. Then she cuddled up to me and we continued to look online for more things to buy. We had a takeaway later on with a bottle of red wine. I hadn't had a takeaway in years but it seemed very natural to her, so I just went with it. To be fair, it was very nice but then anything involving her always is.

Sunday 18th April

We woke up together but she seemed very keen to get home so she left pretty early in the day. I said I would come with her but she skilfully avoided that with logistics. I will see if I can get her address from old HR records at work, or, failing that, I will follow her.

Monday 19th April

Bank Holiday Monday which is good as I hate going to work knowing my darling is free to lie in a little, make coffee and just listen to the radio. Maybe a walk in the cold air and to just generally 'be' is what I need. I want to join her so much and just live like that, with her, simply. Today is how things could be if there was no work in the way.

Work tomorrow and I don't want to go. I've never really felt like this. I think others do all the time, but it's never really bothered me, until now.

Tuesday 20th April

I thought about Dad today for no real reason. I woke up at 4am and he was right there. I feel like my memory of him is slipping away. I feel like I romanticise now that he is gone. I do find there is nothing better for your personal PR than to die. People get better every day after they die. They were kind, generous or 'happy go lucky'. Memories become all misty. I don't forget the reality neither before nor after death, but in my Dad's case, it seems I am complying.

She is coming round tomorrow night for tea. I wonder if she will pick up the conversation about us living together. I am not prepared for that and I still haven't been to where she lives. I don't even know exactly where that is. I must broach that with her.

I think I might give meditation a go as I have been feeling quite irritable recently.

Wednesday 21st April

I went for a walk at lunchtime as the weather was crisp and cold but the rain was holding off. I missed her terribly as we had become used to walking this walk together. It really seemed to sink in today. I had text her to see if she wanted to join me, but she said it felt odd now that she had left and that somebody might see her and she might look like 'a bit sad'. She also said it was a bit far to come just for a walk.

I couldn't fail to notice how every single person it seems, whether on a bus, a train, at lunch or at any spare moment, including walking along, is addicted to a little screen. They look like modern day zombies. They seek attention, they seek likes, affirmation and the currency is volume. I don't value the number of interactions over the depth of them. I am happy being completely in love and engaged with my darling. That's more than enough for me. Who needs 'a like' from a stranger, who needs ten thousand followers, all of whom you don't know one bit?

I got an opportunity to look for her address on somebody else's computer today. People are so trusting, or maybe just so slack in approach. It had already been archived and I was denied access, or rather my colleague was. That is a pain. Anyway, there are other ways of finding out.

She came round in the evening and she looked wonderful but somehow, I felt she was distracted. Maybe we just couldn't quite replicate the feeling of being away in the cottage. A natural low after such a big high. I said I was thinking of buying a new car which was totally untrue and I just plucked it from the air to maybe give us some online shopping to do. It was just something to say really. She didn't seem at all interested anyway. I hope we can re-capture the magic. I feared it was all an angelic one-off. She left quite early too and she didn't even feel the need to make an excuse. I had assumed she would stay for the night. I don't like the way she leaves stuff just lying around and the way she puts dirty things in the sink. She also saw my wedding video on the side as I hadn't properly stored it away from the time that I last watched it. She asked if I wanted to show it to her and I said definitely not. My answer was too resounding, too forceful and it was uncomfortable and created an awkwardness we hadn't shared before. I also noticed her phone beeping a lot again, but I didn't get the opportunity to investigate properly.

Thursday 22nd April

Work is becoming more horrible. It has reached new levels of nonsense ever since we employed these consultants. If they are so brilliant, why don't they go and make millions in their own business? We all know the answer to that. They have expensive haircuts and the same shiny shoes. Pointy and brown. It's an illusion but it has more than worked on those that set the company budget. One said to me 'I'm not a magician' but actually, that is exactly what they are. They peddle illusions as truth. They are magicians, but that is not a good thing.

The train home was cancelled and so it was two busses for me. We really do take most things for granted and our expectations are now sky high. We want everything 'just so' and we want it now and we cannot wait to complain and feel aggrieved when something, anything, doesn't meet that ridiculous expectation. I could hardly believe the attitudes of others just because they had to catch a bus rather than a train, just this once.

Today was the first day for ages that I didn't text her. She didn't text me. I don't want to create a stand-off, a blinking competition though.

My amazon delivery was hidden between my bins when I got home. Quite a risk and a little thrill to finally pick it up and take it inside.

Friday 23rd April

I've been told to book yet more holidays as otherwise I will lose them. My plan is grander. If I don't take them and then I leave, they will have to pay me for them. My colleague said 'I'll have them' as if he were articulating both a stroke of genius or some amazing comedy. He was the only person laughing.

My lunchtime walks feel flat now. It's conflicting as spring is beautiful, perhaps the most beautiful of the four seasons, but I just can't muster the energy to enjoy it. Most people have stopped any sort of lunch break and most people now just eat at their desks and carry on typing. They don't even look at their food. Just gobble, gobble, gobble. That can't be very good for you.

We have spring, with nature bursting out all over and in so many beautiful ways and yet we just look at screens all day.

Saturday 24th April

I might actually get a new car but whenever I look there is too much choice and I don't really have any knowledge. I wish someone would just tell me the one to buy and the best deal. Plus, once you've driven it a few times the novelty wears off and it's just 'your car'. They are all pretty much the same from behind the steering wheel after a few drives. So, I might not bother. The feeling is passing before it has really begun.

I text her to ask her if we are meeting up this weekend. I even dared to ask if I could go to her house. It took her ages to reply, which annoyed me, but then we agreed to meet in the park and feed the ducks. When I saw her, I just felt such sadness, maybe regret. I am not sure what it was. How could I ever think anything but lovely thoughts about my princess, my darling. She looked beautiful in her long coat, her long auburn hair just gently swaying in the spring breeze. We talked and talked and we walked and walked and I felt like we fell in love all over again. I hope that she felt this too. We had the most romantic hug under a big old oak tree and she looked up into my eyes and then I knew we were back where we belong. I took her to her favourite restaurant for dinner and everything was magical again. I asked her back but she said no and that somehow seemed to break our new spell. I said I could go back to hers but she said no again and I couldn't ask anything else as each rejection hurt too much. I said it was fine, of course, but in truth the atmosphere turned instantly and the evening ended awkwardly. Why can't I just go round to her house? What could she possibly have to hide, to be ashamed of, or not want me to see?

Sunday 25th April

I didn't feel able to text her or call her today somehow. I hope nothing is going wrong. Later on, she text me to say sorry she was grumpy, but she wasn't grumpy, she just didn't want us to sleep together and I don't know why. I thought about it for a while and text back 'Don't be sorry, everything is fine x' but then regretted it as I wished I had asked her if everything was fine rather than stating that it was. No reply and so she was not part of my day really.

I did some gardening which was a joy as I planted and tidied and it looked great by the evening. I tried to listen to the radio but every station I tried was unbearable and after I turned it off, I found natures birdsong to be more than enough, beautiful in fact. I enjoyed my own company as I fleetingly thought of her. I wonder where we are heading?

All in all, I had a lovely day. Everyday can be like this after I have left work.

Monday 26th April

I can hardly believe it, but the consultants and the management have decided we need a recruitment drive. There must be some sort of law against this. They say the new structure is now settled (after about three weeks!) and we need to 'buy in' some 'specific skill sets' and 'experience' plus we need some junior members of staff, some apprentices, so we can start to 'grow our own' and to ensure we can build a 'sustainable culture'. It's all just such bollocks, worse than that it was the plan all along. We have over done it on redundancies and we think we can replace the numbers we need at a cheaper cost. Call it what it is you useless charlatans. Useless or calculating? Which is worse? I will have some fun with this though. The redundant staff should get together and bring about an action I reckon. I'll see what she thinks.

Tuesday 27th April

I've stopped walking at lunchtime now almost altogether. It feels a bit lonely. Like something is missing. It was fine before she came with me, and it would be fine now if she never had. Is it better to have walked together than never to have walked at all? Maybe, in turn, I'll miss it and I will start again soon. I hope so as I miss the trees, the birds and the quiet.

She sent me a text asking for us to have a chat later. It said, 'we need a chat x'. I'll try not to read anything into that but thank goodness it is not days away as my mind would run riot.

When she came round, she had baked a cake. It was gorgeous, delicious. She said she wanted to know if I still felt the same about her. I felt cautious as I wondered if she was letting me go first to give her an easy way out. Anyway, I simply told the truth and said yes, totally and absolutely. She seemed relived and I sensed an insecurity I had not seen before which was utterly charming and endearing. She told me that her ex-boyfriend has been texting her again and again and his texts were getting increasingly nasty. I asked to look at them and she showed me. In my view he was abusive after she had replied very politely. She shouldn't have replied at all. I told her not to worry and that I was glad she had shared this with me and we would sort it out together. She seemed comforted. I have absolutely no idea how I will sort it though, but I am on the front foot here as I know him, and he doesn't know me.

She stayed over and when we went to bed we just hugged and cuddled. She fell asleep in my arms, but I could tell underneath she was scared and that I made her feel safe. That brought about a protective anger in me that I hadn't felt before which was quickly followed by my own fear as I have no idea how to deal with this and I hate confrontation. For all I know he could be a bodybuilder or a boxer or a drug dealer or all three. I need to know more about him. I need to work this one out carefully.

Wednesday 28th April

I text her on the way in about the consultant's idea to bring in new staff so soon after making so many redundant, but she said she didn't care and that she had moved on and that I should just leave it alone. I reminded her that there could well be another pay-off here but she couldn't have been less interested. Then I realised and imagined she was still probably worried about her ex, so I told her that I love her and couldn't wait to see her again. She replied with one solitary kiss 'x'. That's not enough for me to know anything.

Thursday 29th April

I was involved in a meeting today about strategy and I just couldn't help myself. I asked them if they had fully considered all the implications of recruiting so soon after the round of recent redundancies. As this was nothing to do with the meeting it seemed to throw them somewhat. The really slippery one said something about 'parking' that somewhere and coming back to it in an 'appropriate forum'. I said he'd better. He played nervously with his hair as he said it, so round one to me chump.

She is coming round for her tea tonight and I hope she stays over as that always makes me feel like we are more real somehow and that we get to spend more quality time together. The times when we are silent, just there, with no need to talk are the very best moments. I'll ask more about the ex-boyfriend and then I can start to cook up my plan to rid her of him.

Why hasn't she invited me round to her house yet? *It is on my mind.*

Friday 30th April

A text from Ms Hinchcliffe this morning, asking me about her iPad and Wi-Fi. No texts at all about important matters, or how I am, or what I might be doing but as soon as her iPad is interrupted, she is straight at me. I told her to text her daughter as I am busy but she text back, without any hint of irony, to say that my sister doesn't know how to fix such things. I'll make her wait as it is all too painful to try and fix such things over the phone and I am damned if I am driving all that way for her and her first world problem.

After my darling decided not to stay last night, I had a notion to follow her home but it felt wrong. Maybe I could try again to find out her address. Why hasn't she invited me round to hers yet? However, maybe first, I will concentrate on this ex-boyfriend.

When I arrived home from work, there was a perfect spiders web at the front door. It was truly a thing of beauty. Unfortunately, it could not survive me opening the door as the spider had placed it right on the opening. I felt sorry for it and I felt sad when I opened the door. I took a picture of it first on my phone to keep. I wondered if this might be what our defence against the machines will amount to. We will be the spider.

She came round again this evening and I feel like we are really back on track. She asked if she could stay over and it was so endearing that she felt she even needed to ask. We opened a bottle of wine and we did talk about her ex-boyfriend. I got a few details, just enough to go on but not enough to implicate myself too deeply. I'll start the research, but I'll do it very carefully. I cannot leave a trace.

I'd do anything for her. Anything. *I'll keep you safe my darling.*

Saturday 1st May

I didn't sleep too well and I felt we were fighting for territory in bed a little. Now I feel irritated by today somehow. Months should not begin on a Saturday. Ms Hinchcliffe insists I go over today to sort her iPad out. Not a chance I am dancing to that tune. Perhaps I am a little lost and without plan. My darling left early and I doubt I will see her again today so perhaps I will go to Ms Hinchcliffe's after all. I can use her iPad then for research on my foe and I don't have to take my darling to meet her.

I made a cup of coffee and noticed a new spiders web at the window. I didn't disturb it and felt comforted to think it was a replacement for yesterday's front door one. The same spider I thought, maybe. I also saw two pigeons on my lawn. I'm not fond of pigeons. I don't know who is. I banged on the window but they are nothing if not blasé. They left eventually, but on their own terms.

I went over to Ms Hinchcliffe's as my darling confirmed she couldn't meet again later today but that we would meet tomorrow, so I will make her a lovely lunch. The iPad took me about two minutes to fix but I pretended it took longer and got some useful information on the ex. The internet is so helpful and people tell you everything on social media. I'll drop by his address on my way back to have a look at where he lives. *Yes, let's see you sonny.*

Sunday 2nd May

We had a lovely lunch together and we just chatted. I love it when she smiles, or giggles at my jokes. She asked me to read a book she enjoyed and so I will. I am particular about reading matter, so I hope she has good taste. I've never heard of it.

After she left, I decided to start a fire in my back garden today to get rid of a few things. I bought a proper burning bin from the garden centre and some fuel, but the fire lit a treat on its own. Dry paper is a perfect fuel. I followed an urge and I threw my wedding video in for good measure when the fire was at its most aggressive and the pleasure of this evil somehow forced a smile onto my lips as I saw it die forever in the flames. It gave off a foul smelling black smoke as its final message to me and the world but it is gone now. *Fire is so destructive, isn't it, so useful?*

It was a bonfire of my vanities.

I feel ready for next week somehow. I am in charge.

Monday 3rd May

It's May Day but I volunteered to work and now I feel more fed up of this bus and train journey than ever. I can't think why I did volunteer. Still, the same old faces in their old, crumpled clothes joined me. There must be more to life than this. Perhaps not much more. But just maybe there is and just maybe I am about to explore it. I used my travel time to think about my new foe again. How to eradicate him from her life without getting too close or implicating myself. My clean criminal record is helpful here as no one would ever suspect me of petty crimes such as damaging his property. I haven't had the idea yet, but it will arrive. Necessity is the mother of invention.

I text my darling on the way home, but she took a while to reply. *Where is she?* Not working seems to suit her and all the stress has left her beautiful body and face but surely she should be more available to me now and she knows my travel times, so why does it take so long to text me back? It turned out she has had received even more texts from him and they are more aggressive and threatening now. She asked if we should tell the police. *Be careful texting my dear, as it all creates a trail.* I said maybe we should, but we absolutely will not as we don't want to shine a light on ourselves. The issue is clearly becoming more urgent. I offered that she come and stay at mine for a few days so that she couldn't be in if he did call. He knows nothing of me so she would be completely safe. She said that might be a good idea. *Might?*

Tuesday 4th May

No call from the premium bonds people yesterday so I'll stick with 'plan A', whatever that is. People are obsessed with planning, more so than doing. Always fixating on a point in the future where everything will come together. *It won't.*

An emergency call from my darling in the middle of the morning though took me somewhat by surprise. He turned up at her house and was banging on the door. She panicked but luckily she mustered just enough composure to hide. He was shouting through the letterbox. This has clearly upset her and understandably so. I told her to pack a bag and I would pick her up after work, but she was clearly too frightened to wait so I made a polite excuse and left work there and then. How brave, how maverick of me. People seemed a bit shocked as I have never needed to do anything like that before. I even took a taxi home to speed up the process. It cost a fortune but who cares. I had the added benefit of seeing her house and finally knowing more about where she lives. She left out of the back door and met me a few doors down. Her house looked perfectly respectable to me, a mid-terrace, so maybe there is nothing in that at all, maybe she just prefers mine as it is bigger. Anyway, she looked so frightened and also so pleased to see me, her protector. *Don't worry darling, this will all be over soon. I'll make sure of that.*

Wednesday 5th May

She's with me now, night and day. I have to admit I felt a bit freaked out when I left her in the house on her own this morning. I've never had such a sensation. She could root through anything and everything when I am not there. My mind went into overdrive as to what she could find, or disturb, or judge. I said I needed some shopping but she said she didn't want to go out and I understood that. I took the car into work and whilst the car parking will be an astronomical cost, it saves me time both sides so I could leave a little later in the morning and I'll be home a little earlier in the evening. However, without saying anything to her, I took the chance on the way home to drive by his house. I parked outside but across the street. I was lucky enough to see him just mooching about. I got a good sense of him and then I drove home.

Thursday 6th May

It is a bit suffocating to have someone with you all of the time at home. I didn't realise this would be so. I have become so used to living alone. She asked me to take her back to her house to pick up some more stuff and I said of course, and that I would go in with her but then I saw quite the reaction. A real push back against me going inside. It is not in my imagination, she doesn't want me to see *something, to be in there.* She doesn't want me inside her house. But why? I felt a touch angry this time about it.

I do need my own space, some silence. I need to breathe and be on my own sometimes. I love her but I hadn't considered this properly. Anyway, it's not like she has *moved in* so hopefully all will resolve itself soon. Maybe I will just get used to it.

Friday 7th May

My sister called me late last night. She sounded drunk. *She was drunk.* Eventually I asked her outright if she had been drinking and she admitted it through a confessional slur of speech. She isn't supposed to drink so there is every chance she is doing herself even more harm. I expect, in time, that will be my fault. Anyway, the wine went in and the truth came out. She hates me apparently. *For what I have done to her!* Except of course she means, technically, for what I haven't done, or refused to do. She hates me because I didn't give her any money to speed up her treatment. Her operation has been delayed. By that logic everyone who needs to go to hospital for any type of procedure has full authority to hate me as I didn't pay for them either. I didn't hold back this time. I asked her why she felt entitled to my money. All she kept saying was that I was close family, that we were flesh and blood. Does that count for anything if you don't keep in touch, if you don't even like each other? Am I lacking compassion? I would do anything for my darling, so I decided that I had made the right decision. She told me she might die due to the delay, but I felt that was just wine induced drama. I can't carry that sort of guilt. I told her we all have to die someday. The call didn't end well. It spoilt my journey into work this morning as I couldn't stop thinking about it. Everyone else seemed predictably chipper given that it is Friday. I reckon you can tell what day of the week it is just from the expression of people on public transport. Set me aside, people are the same everywhere.

Also, I worked out my plan for the ex-boyfriend, but even here, in my own diary I had better not share. Just to be on the safe side.

Saturday 8th May

I think we had our first row today. I think it was purely a combination of me feeling a little bit trapped in my own house and her anxiety about her ex-boyfriend. I can't even remember what the trigger was but luckily she felt worse than I did so I pushed home this advantage by apologising first. We had a lovely chat afterwards and a cuddle in front of the television. She introduced me to various films and box sets and when I picked one, I soon hoped I had accidently picked the runt of the litter as it was awful, just dreadful and sickly and I had no idea why she liked it or laughed at its ridiculousness. Just so corny and predictable, and as if written from a template or by a bot of some sort. Anyway, I pretended it was okay, given the strain of the day, but I wasn't really watching it anyway as I was just stroking her hair and feeding her Maltesers. She is so beautiful. I am happy to watch her watching trash as long as she is in my lap.

I didn't dare raise going to her house again and actually going inside as I didn't want to risk sparking another row.

Sunday 9th May

The weather was so good to us today, and so we were able to spend most of the day in the garden. She is a good gardener, tidy, efficient and with a good eye for form and colour. I had no need to supervise and her input was very welcome. Although her suggestions to overhaul a whole area started to grate after a while. *Leave it alone my darling, it is fine.* It was nice to be outside all day. Peaceful. In life, our expectation of nature is basically zero so we are always delighted by what nature brings. We simply accept it as sort of 'god given'. That's why we love it so much. That's why people can just sit and stare or listen to waterfalls all day long.

Isn't technology wonderful. I managed to get more than a few minutes today alone with my darling's phone. I dutifully sent her to the shops having hidden it behind a cushion. I made her go, told her it would be good for her to go out alone and see she had nothing to worry about. She complied given it was for her own good. This allowed me more than enough time to download a tracker onto her phone. It will not only give me knowledge of her location, but it will be quite handy I believe and I justified it as a safety measure given the threat of her ex-boyfriend. If she ever finds out, I can play innocent and say I was just really concerned in case I ever needed to know where she was in a hurry. *You can't be too careful, my darling.* It was so easy to research and install. Child's play. It makes you wonder just how free we all are now. Every movement, every noise can be monitored. Surely, at least, we are still able to think without invasion. One day that will no doubt end too.

Later on, I wished I has looked more deeply at her contacts, messages, email and pictures. Maybe I missed an opportunity, but there will be others.

Monday 10th May

I really didn't want to go to work today. The sun was still shining in through the window, the bed was just so comfy and warm and she was laying beautifully beside me. It felt like another Sunday. My muscles ached from all the gardening and I was close to throwing my first ever 'sickie' but something inside me prevented me from following through. We all have a deep routed moral compass that seems to govern us when it really matters. More's the pity.

On the journey in, it still felt like Sunday, I just couldn't shake it. Why is the weather so important? Somehow everything seemed slower and calmer and sitting at my desk in the office just felt wrong. I idled through the day with the minimum of effort and I called my darling at lunchtime. She said she had continued gardening without me and I felt so sad yet so happy. She said I had some interesting post, whatever that means, and she then said she had another text asking where she was. He is beginning to enrage me. I told her to try meditation and to turn her phone off after she hung up. I bet she didn't do either. Well, I know she didn't as I could still see her exact location.

I went home as soon as I could and she had prepared dinner which was simple but fantastic. As I ate it, the robin sat on the window sill as if carrying out some kind of audit on us. As brazen as you like it just sat there. It made us both smile and chuckle. I was full of gratitude and love all evening.

Tuesday 11th May

Tuesday's are the worst day of the working week. Last weekend is far enough gone and the next one is too far away. If the weather is bad, that makes it worse. It rained, which pleased me a bit as the garden needs it now that we have worked on it. How old have I become?

Not too long now until my share option matures.

On the way home I considered the possibility of moving to Devon. We both could sell up, I will be leaving work and we could just go and live down there. It would be like our holiday but all of the time. No ex-boyfriends, old friends or guilty memories to bother us then. All the baggage and history just left behind us. The thought filled me with joy. I'll roll it around in my mind and then I might suggest it at the weekend. I need to look at property prices down there too. The thought of just fleeing to Devon, or somewhere.

When I got home, I just couldn't stop myself. I shared my idea. I've never seen a smile that big. She seemed so happy, as if all of the weight she had ever carried in her mind had simply lifted. We cuddled on the sofa and looked at properties. We had no restrictions. She didn't even ask about work. We found loads and imagined living in them, what we would do to improve the house, where we would put things and what we might need to buy. We explored local areas and planned walks and pub lunches. This was so much more than my heart could hold. She is all mine. She makes me feel like whenever we are together, I could not grow old.

When we went to bed, she quickly fell asleep and I just watched her in the half light and listened to her gentle sleeping noises. Little crackles and whimpers. So beautiful.

Nobody knows when their life will end and so what exactly did I take, what exactly did I steal? Nothing, that's what.

Wednesday 12th May

I didn't want to leave her this morning I wanted last evening and night to simply continue. It won't be too long now. No more texts from the old boyfriend, maybe he has given up? That would be great, but I'll prepare for the worst whilst hoping for the best.

Someone in the office asked if I was still in touch with her. Ha! still in touch! I ask you! Maybe the gossip lines aren't what they once were now some have left. I said yes, we are still in touch, and I tried to supress my grin with little success. Still in touch! Oh yes. *She is all mine.*

Thursday 13th May

Last night my princess asked me what I thought of the book she had asked me to read as had told her I would read it during my commute. I scanned through it as, after reading the first two pages, I was embarrassed that it had ever reached my hand. I also considered that someone would see what I was reading and I didn't want to represent myself that way in public. Anyway, I told her I was halfway through it and that it wasn't what I usually read and so it was a nice change. She said she loved the romance in it. Hopefully she won't ask again.

At work today they asked me why certain task haven't been done. I said the lady who used to do them no longer works here as you 'ended her'. That's the phrase I used, that's exactly what I said. Ended her. I tried not to chuckle but I'm too happy at the moment to play deadpan. Not only did they say that they expected me to pick up those tasks now but also, to punch the bruise, that I needed to work back from when they were last done. I asked which current tasks they wanted me to relinquish to allow me to do that. They rolled their eyes. I asked them to think about it and 'get back to me'. Later on, I found out that they had asked someone else instead to pick up the tasks. Idiots everywhere.

My darling text me during the day to tell me I had some 'interesting post'. She seems to think all post is interesting. Last time it was a bank statement so this time it might well be a flyer.

Friday 14th May

I'm happy it is Friday again, although my morning was interrupted by a text from Ms Hinchcliffe. Yes, she who changes her will but doesn't tell you what was in it originally nor what is in the newly amended version. I'm less inclined to act as some sort of remote butler until I know I'm getting my fair share. Well, that and all the years of no love and emotional neglect. *I am owed.* It was father who built up the wealth anyway, not her. He was the worker, the grafter who unassumedly toiled for years just to move her up the social and property ladder. He always seemed in her debt, somehow. He gave her his life and she now just sits there with zero gratitude and then she has the nerve, the audacity to remove his memory and change her name. It took me many years to recognise and get over my childhood, and now my father has departed I can see her for what she is. Selfish and rude. *So, your little demands by text can indeed wait.*

When I returned home, I was a little saddened and surprised to hear that my darling wants to try and go and live back at her house for a while. I had mixed feelings as I like my own space and I have found her to be unintentionally intrusive, but I also don't want to lose her now. As we were talking my phone beeped again so I explained it was a text from Ms Hinchcliffe. That caused some confusion which we cleared up quickly but now she wants to meet both my mother and sister. I told her we are not close, but stupidly revealed that my sister is ill. She does not yet know I declined her funding request. Now she seems even more intent to meet them. Hopefully this will just blow away like the leaves in Autumn. The real issue is just how I feel about my darling moving back into her own house again. Do I want her here? Is she safe there? *Will we feel further apart?*

Saturday 15th May

As we drove over to her house, she asked again about meeting Ms Hinchcliffe and my sister. I said 'let's see' or some such trivial, deflective reply. *Please give up on this one my love, they are not good enough for you.*

She asked me to drop her at the end of the road but there was no chance of me accepting this and so I dropped her outside. *I was driving.* I said it was silly that I couldn't come in, but she seemed to both take offence at this as well as becoming immediately sad. It almost felt like shame. With some loathing, I agreed and watched her approach the door. She looked as nervous and as timid as a kitten. She went inside and offered the faintest of waves. Something compelled me to wait. Maybe I wanted to see if the ex-boyfriend would appear. Had he been watching us arrive? Was he here? Had I given him an advantage by being here and being seen? It occurred to me in that moment that I could have made a real schoolboy error. Even as those thoughts were working their way through, she bolted back out of the front door with a shriek. She ran towards me. She looked so frightened and childlike. I had never seen her like this. Oddly, part of it all revulsed me. She almost pulled the car door handle off. When she finally got in her breathing was so fast that she couldn't speak. Eventually she said, 'It's him, he's been in' and I knew without hesitation what we were facing. As we entered her house together, I was met with destruction and vandalism of the pettiest type. Graffiti on the walls, curtains pulled down and the like. He wanted her to feel his presence, his rage. He was exerting control. A control he is not entitled to and doesn't have. *I shall take this from him.* I made a solemn promise to myself at that moment, and it is one I will, without question, keep.

However, this unfortunate turn of events had, at last, gained me access to her house, so I was pleased with that. She also agreed it was better to come back to mine, with me, tonight.

Sunday 16th May

I don't think either of us slept but we both pretended to. I asked her if she would like a coffee in bed and she said yes. I made her feel safe, I reminded her that he has no idea where she is and he couldn't even look for her at work. I don't know that for certain as I took an uncalculated risk in driving to hers, but the probability is that he wouldn't be just hanging around all the while, especially after he had just broken into her house. She only partly believed me and that pain I saw in her eyes is something I have to resolve. *I cannot have my darling in pain.* She said she must call the police, but I talked her out of it. *We don't want the attention my love, as the key events are yet to come.* I said we could fix it all. She said she wouldn't be able to claim on the insurance if she didn't call the police. I said I would pay. *Who cares about money?* She eventually said she loved me and after the coffee she fell asleep. *There is, of course, my darling, one more conversation that we need to have. You are avoiding it. You are hoping I didn't see, but I did.*

It was much later when we talked properly again. In the meantime, I had been considering my mental 'to do' list which had been re-ordered during the day thanks to a change in urgency and priority. *I must deal with the most important matters first.*

It was quite late when I finally confronted her. 'I saw' I simply said. My voice was soft. She didn't, from that point on offer any resistance. 'Oh' she said. *Oh indeed.* I asked her to explain. I could see her considering a lie which offended me no end, but I waited and my patience paid off. I didn't feel anywhere near as shocked as I might have and it was all such a long time ago. She has a child from a teenage pregnancy. She was just fifteen and she has no contact with the father whatsoever. Why she just couldn't hide the pictures and let me in I don't know? Easy, but there we are. That is why I couldn't go into her house. I have to say it does offer some practical difficulties but other than that I asked about him, the son. She told me the whole story. Their separation at birth, their reunion. He seems to be doing okay for himself in the grand scheme of things and he is grown up now so maybe it is all something and nothing. In one sense anyway. I asked her how much contact she has with her son and she just said they are 'in touch' and meet every now and again. She says they are treading carefully but getting ever closer. Her feelings are complex as she explained she has never really felt like his mother, and she has never since been a mother again. She says it feels more like awkward friends, but she is grateful for that over nothing. I dared to ask how does he feel about her? She said she honestly didn't know but maybe he also doesn't really regard her as his Mum. It was clearly very upsetting and distressing for her to explain this all to me. She says the big conversations have been done and are over. I said I would meet him with her if she liked and she seemed to see this as a huge act of commitment at the same time as having a big weight lifted from her shoulders. She seemed so relieved but it honestly wasn't such a big deal to me. She hugged me so hard I couldn't breathe. She cried and said I was truly wonderful. She had clearly been hiding a shame that affected her deeply but I couldn't see the shame, only circumstance. Eventually I felt the relief of a mystery uncovered but also felt determined to bring another episode of her life to its end. One thing really felt like no big deal to me and the other feels like a big deal indeed. This is the opposite of how she saw things and that is quite helpful.

Monday 17th May

I booked tomorrow of work which annoys me as it is, to a degree, a record of my whereabouts. Hopefully the links are too tenuous for anyone ever to spot them.

When I got home, I made the mistake of telling her to wait before beginning the to repair her house. *Concentrate! no trail, remember.* I had to make up a reason why.

Tuesday 18th May

I left as if going to work as normal this morning and made an excuse as to why I needed to take the car. I walked down his street door by door with my car tucked away out of sight and with some sort of half disguise on. Just a hat and a scarf around my lower face really. Thankfully the weather was just cold enough to justify this. Enough.

I knocked on every door *(not really)* to give the illusion of credibility and then I got to his house. He was in and my official sounding voice and his absolute lack of suspicion or any possible recognition got me into his house easily. He was quite a rough looking character. He looked quite strong though. He looked like he used to play sport but has now given up on himself. A smoker as well. Disgusting. He seemed the lazy type to me. *Oh, why princess, what made you want to be with him?* I imagined he might have been different long ago. I offered trust by telling him I found a fiver and giving it back to him. The smallest price to pay. He even offered me a cup of tea. *Not for me. I don't want to leave a trace.* I told him, quite quickly that I had finished for now, but I would have to call back and asked when he would be in. *I am to call back on Thursday. Can I do this in my lunch hour?* I'm going to have to, as then I will have work as my alibi. I needed to arrange the follow up visit quickly as I cannot risk being intercepted by any contact with the real gas board or supplier. I am quite a good actor. I enjoy knowing what he doesn't know, I rather revelled in my position of power and enjoyed the fact that he is completely clueless and so easy to fool. *You simply do not find what you are not looking for.* I will probably need to burn this diary at some point. I am getting rather accomplished at burning. *He is in my pocket.*

When I saw her in the evening, her fear of living acted as a spur I barely needed. The plan is set and I will execute it perfectly, just like I always do. It is not a fair fight and so only I can win. It is just what he deserves. Part of me will enjoy this, the other part will be just scared enough to fully focus and concentrate on the details of my plan. My schedule is tight, my plan is efficient yet laced with danger.

Wednesday 19th May

Today was a huge day. So much adrenalin and such a need to hide it. I went in to work. I made sure I spoke to just about all of my colleagues, but not in an obvious way. I took the bus and train but had already left my car where I needed it the evening before. She didn't notice a thing. Now it was all just about bravery and execution.

At lunchtime I causally left work. I got a taxi to nearby, but not too near, his house. I paid cash and made no attempt to connect at all with the driver. It was booked under 'Wilde'. I got out and strode with assurance to his door. *I had an appointment!* but only verbally, which was perfect. I just needed to hold my nerve and nobody would suspect anything. My research on gas and method has been done on the PC's of others. *Nothing comes back to me.* There is no trail back to me as long as I could get back to work on time and not arouse any suspicion or questions. The idiot welcomed me in with open arms. He seemed scruffier today, gruff even. A slob. I'm sure he was wearing the same clothes as last time. Yuk. No time to gloat, stay focused. I used the thought of his texts and his raid on her home, the invasion of her sanctuary, as motivation. I even imagined them together once and I instantly had more than enough drive to finish this job. We chatted a little and he asked me if I wanted a cup of tea again. Not a chance. I never took my gloves off. I wore new shoes that I would dispose of. I asked him to sit in the living room and close the door so he wouldn't inhale any escaped gas. Of course, the opposite was true, I was trapping him in his cocoon of poison. As he sat there, his lungs filled and he slid away. It was so quick, so much quicker than I expected, but I am no expert in these matters. *A bonus.* Too easy. He trusted me. *I had him there, right in the palm of my hand.* Almost too easy. For no reason I played with his nose, but I quickly regained focus. I smothered him to his timely death, just to make certain, and then I opened up the gas as if there had been some sort of accident. I just needed to get out of there and then the whole thing would go up in flames. I left and nobody saw me. *People do not find what they are not looking for.* I didn't hear the explosion but knew it would come. I took my car back to work and I arrived back in good time and acted as naturally as I could. I waited and waited for news of the explosion without ever looking for it online. I just waited and just as I was becoming more and more anxious, the news broke. *A major house fire, police and fire services at the scene.* I knew it might be a day or two before they could declare it all a terrible accident and name the dead. I sat there and quietly ate my tuna sandwich. I also hoped the neighbours would be okay.

I set off for home a little later than usual to make it look like I had taken my usual train and bus. I was careful and it all went like clockwork.

Thursday 20th May

Trying not to mention one of my proudest achievements to anyone is proving difficult. Why do we seek recognition from others so much? Why do we feel the need to gloat, to gain the praise of others? In the long term, my approach will make everything just so. *Hold your nerve, hold your nerve. We will be free as birds soon my angel.*

A new scheme was introduced at work today. Surely another one of the consultant ideas. You now get your birthday off as holiday. However, our annual holiday entitlement has been reduced by one day. So, the benefit, the scheme, the latest motivational tool, is to force you to take one of your holiday days on your birthday. Genius. I asked them, what if your birthday falls on a Saturday or what if you were born on the 29th February and they soon gave up trying to answer. I have no doubt we will all be sent a balloon or something too and will be asked to post it on LinkedIn.

Friday 21st May

At last, just what was needed. The call from my darling finally arrived. I answered nonchalantly. She was in high panic. Had I heard? *Heard what my love?* Did I know? *Know what my princess?* She said her ex-boyfriend had been found dead at his house. A terrible accident. A gas leak apparently. He had been unconscious before the explosion apparently. Terrible news I said. It was all going so beautifully until she said the police wanted to speak to her. She asked if I would be there. *I most certainly will, I said.* I asked for some immediate compassionate leave and it was granted. I could see me becoming the new gossip fodder as I departed. People hushed and drew breath as I left. They pulled that face, the one that says, 'I am feeling for you' but all you can see was 'I'm glad it's not me' plus *'Can I have all the juicy details?'* Two plus two makes ten, especially at work. But not even they could guess the real story. I told them I would take care of her. *Such a nice guy they all thought.* Ah bless.

On the way home I called her to say perhaps best not to mention his break in at her house as it would complicate things and they would probably ask why she hadn't reported it in the first place. This spooked her in just the right measure, and she agreed all too easily. Therefore, this should be a breeze, I thought.

Two officers came round. Very official looking. One man, one woman. Deep, concerned voices. *Just as they are trained.* I offered them tea, but they declined and then the chap said, somewhat out from behind his character, 'Oh, go on then'. The female one didn't seem to approve. I think she was the boss.

They asked about the relationship. *'Over years ago Sir',* she said. They asked what he was like. *'Don't really know, no real contact Sir',* she said. They asked if I had ever met him. *'Sorry, no Sir',* I said. They asked more inane questions before confirming they just had to 'explore and establish all the circumstances' before they could conclude their report. Easy as that. *'It was all a terrible accident, Sir'.* She cried a bit for good measure and I pulled my best faces.

She seemed shook up by the whole thing, so I had to pretend to be shaken too. I did say, perhaps too early in the process, that at least she could sleep easy now and get on with her life. I'll gently re-enforce this message as time passes but it was way too soon for me to say that. Seed planted though. *You are free of him now princess, we are free of the burden of your past mistakes.*

Saturday 22nd May

We were having such a lovely day when the police called again. We had been planning the garden and talking about sorting her house out when we were rudely disturbed. They want to talk to my lovely again. They said she could come to the station if she preferred or that they could ask their questions at the house. We stayed put.

I've been thinking, and it's been waking me up a bit. I want to know more about her child's father. She must know his name, or something about him. I mean, they were fully intimate at least once. Or maybe, as she was so young, he was a predator. *Now that would change things.*

The police questioning didn't go as well as I had hoped. They seemed more probing and one of them was plain clothed. They were asking about recent contact, *they were asking about motive*. Of course, I must remember my darling is innocent. She just wouldn't have it in her, *surely they can see that*. She did rather bluster about them being in touch and she still didn't say anything about the break-in. *Good girl, hold tight and everything will be okay*. They asked where she was on the date and at the time of the explosion. She said at mine. They asked if anyone was with her. I wanted to say me, but we hadn't planned it. I'd said I was at work anyway, all day. He asked if she had popped to the shops or maybe seen a neighbour, but she just shook her head. She had been too scared to go out but she couldn't tell them why. *Not great*. Then they asked why she wasn't at her own home. *Don't you dare bring that house into it. No, you cannot go there!* Still, that was an easy one to answer. *We are in love officer.*

I knew they couldn't possibly have any evidence at all of her being there because I know for certain that she wasn't. They seemed to get a little more heavy handed so I pushed back a little. I said she was being very helpful at a very traumatic time and asked if they had concluded their questions. They left. They seemed more inquisitive than I would have liked, they left almost disappointed. It was not a great exchange. Some holes to be filled but you cannot backtrack once a truth or a lie has been stated.

That night, as we dined, she was not in a great place. She said it was horrible and she couldn't get the accident out of her head. She said she had visions of him burning to death. I said it would have been quick, instant but that just seemed to bring new pictures into her imagination. So, I said he was probably asleep and didn't know anything about it. *In the middle of the day?* I told her that grieving is natural and that we would never wish any other person harm and so her feelings are totally understandable. She said I was lovely, and caring. *Yes, darling, I am.*

Sunday 23rd May

The police were back again and this time asked to see her phone. She showed them it without hesitation. She had left the messages on it between them. *A stupid mistake, I thought that was too obvious to mention.* I had assumed she had simply deleted them. One finger swipe from absolution. They took her phone in a little see through bag. She was beside herself. They said they would be back in touch. I told her some text messages proved nothing but she says they will think she lied about not having contact with him. I told her to just tell them she was scared. But not so far as to say so scared that she might ever think about any kind of retribution. She looked at me in a new way. I told her we needed to clean her house up without delay. The rest of the day and evening was unsettled at best and I was glad to get to bed, but she disturbed my sleep terribly.

Monday 24th May

I left her sleeping in bed and so I text her from the train and then stupidly realised she doesn't have her phone. We rely on them so much these days. I imagined my text alert going off in that little clear plastic bag in some police station cupboard and it made me laugh. People looked at me as you are not ever supposed to laugh on the train or on any public transport or perhaps at all anymore.

When I got into the office, I called her on my landline and thankfully she answered. I could barely remember the number. She is going to go to the house and make a start. I said I would come after work and see how she is getting on. I told her to buy a 'pay as you go' phone for the interim but she didn't seem keen and says she doesn't know anybody's number anyway, as they are all just stored and saved in her usual phone. I told her to concentrate on the graffiti and the signs of him. Make it look like normal decorating as quickly as possible. She said nothing, she seemed a little stunned.

When I got to her house, quite late on, it looked as though she had barely made a start at all. She seemed to be picking at edges rather than getting on with it properly. I told her I would book Wednesday off as I have loads of holidays still and then we could go at it fully together. She looked so pale and weak. So helpless. I felt a bit sorry for her and felt a desire to protect and comfort her. She said she didn't know what she would do without me, so I reassured her she would never have to think about that again and that I would always be there. The graffiti is awful, I've no idea how you remove that, I suppose we can just paint over it. The house doesn't look all that damaged really, just disturbed and graffitied really.

I carefully put the bins out. One or two items were placed in neighbours' bins at the very last minute. It will be more of a relief than usual to see that truck tomorrow. The shoes are the big thing I reckon, forensically speaking.

Tuesday 25th May

I submitted my request for a day off and it was granted but I am now told that the new rule is that they expect five days notice. They also made comment about my compassionate leave saying that I had 'the benefit of more than a typical amount usually'. I didn't raise to it. I mean it's not as if I can help people dying is it. That thought did make me chuckle. *They die, they die and I get a day off.*

Wednesday 26th May

We got up early and went to the DIY store and then made a real start on her house. We had no idea what to buy but we gave each other enough confidence to suggest that we knew what we were doing so we bought turps, paint, cleaning fluids, cloths and some containers and buckets. When we arrived, we had a lovely attitude and mood about us.

Our morning was interrupted by a visiting police car and Mister plain clothes and his dumb assistant both knocked on the door. I knew that this would look bad, but we had to style this one out. *Don't lie I said.*

When they came in and started talking, you could see them gawping at the walls and the mess as they asked her questions. I'd just about covered the graffiti up but it was still a state. I did feel from very early on like they were building to some sort of crescendo. I am not sure if the state of the house tipped the balance with them or not but events turned.

They explained that someone had visited his house on the day. *How did they know that?* Did she have any idea who? *How could she?* There has been no forced entry, so it must have been some one he knew. *It wasn't, think cleverer!* They asked why she had lied about having no contact with him. She said she was scared. Why was she scared of him they asked? Because he is a bully and can, on occasion, be violent. *Too far and a mistake my darling. Too much rope.*

The texts, the lies and the house all led to them taking her to the station for further questioning. She wasn't arrested but this was a mess. Without me there, she might crumble and implicate herself. My breathing tightened. But she didn't do anything I exclaimed, she is completely innocent. It fell on deaf ears. After she left, I did have a little cry. A cry that signalled some stupid police officers choosing to hurt my darling unnecessarily. I needed to think, to work out how to protect her. There was one truly obvious way, but there is no benefit in that. Plus, just, *no way*.

I got busy with cleaning and painting the house to give me distraction and the space to think.

They let her go, really late on though and luckily they allowed her to have her phone back and so she could call me, and I picked her up. She looked so fragile and weak. She hadn't eaten. They had asked her the same questions over again. I said they couldn't possibly have evidence of something she didn't do. She said they focussed on her lying about contact, on the state of the house and on the fact nobody could vouch for where she was. They made her plot a timeline and made her feel guilty for being in my house all day and not seeing anybody else. All circumstantial I said. Lots of theory but no evidence could ever surface because she was nothing to do with this. *I can be fully certain of that.* I told her to focus on the fact she had done nothing wrong. She asked me whether I totally believed her, and I said I did, without question. *One hundred percent, my darling.*

She insisted she stay at her house for a few days so I drove her back there. That is my fault as I had planted the seed that she is safe now he is gone. I tried to convince her to stay with me but she was insistent. I'll let her stay there, feel scared, and she'll be back with me in no time.

Thursday 27th May

To say my head wasn't in work today was a massive understatement.

People are predisposed to believing the written word. It comes from a time, not all that long ago, when the written word had some sanctity, sacredness and inherent dignity. The written word, until quite recently, generally had some authority, some validation. Nowadays anyone can write anything and anyone else can read it.

Our brains don't seem to have caught up with that. We need to do that quickly. I do put some faith in the younger generation, they seem, paradoxically, smarter and more used to this new world yet also they are also the ones most suffering within it.

Friday 28th May

It is Ms Hinchcliffe's birthday tomorrow and so naturally she didn't want to see me on the actual day. *Turns out she herself won't see the actual day either.* I didn't tell my princess about the birthday as she would have insisted even more strongly on joining me and obviously, I didn't want that.

I finished work early today as some sort of 'new reward' so headed over earlier then I had planned. As I arrived, she was discourteous and insolent. *Telling me this, telling me that.* Directing me as if I were somehow under her control. I swapped her pills and quite quickly she fell asleep in her chair with her hot tea steaming away yet growing ever colder. I just sat and looked at her for a while. I considered the total lack of love. I considered her and Dad and wondered why he had ever become a two with her in the first place. They never seemed happy and she always seemed to have the upper hand. Like master and servant. I considered how and why he had given her so much time, so much of himself. A quiet anger grew inside me. Even though she was a sitting duck, frail and weak and helpless, I could still only see a vindicative old woman for whom I had no love, only scorn. It wasn't difficult, neither mechanically nor emotionally. *It was an act of mercy.* Before I did it, I looked in her polished chestnut bureau to find her last will and testament and there, placed right there, at the top, it sat as if it were there for me to discover. The envelope was unsealed and clearly labelled. It felt official, it gave the illusion of authority and it had been drawn up by the local solicitor. *So, no chance of alteration, more's the pity.* To my horror, yet somehow without surprise, I discovered three main beneficiaries all apportioned in different measure. Firstly, a full fifty percent to my sister. Thirty percent to the local dog's home and just twenty percent to me. It continued to articulate how my sister had first dibs on all personal effects. First refusal and seniority as a child. She didn't even like dogs that much as far as I knew. The rage I felt was only overtaken by the total justification and calmness of what I was about to do. Oh yes, means, opportunity and now motive gave me a sense of purpose, a sense of duty almost. My composure intensified as I thought about how to gently ensure the job was done without anyone ever suspecting anything of me. Nobody knows I am even here, I thought, and I had parked my car far enough away for the neighbours not to see. They won't see what they are not looking for. Twenty percent is better than nothing, but if I take it now, it gives me time to make up for the minor share on offer and who knows I might get more when and if my sister does die. Nobody thought anything of it. Nobody. Easy as pie. *One more makes no difference really, does it?*

Saturday 29th May

Life doesn't complete, it just ends. So, enjoy the party. Has anyone found her yet? I wonder who will tell me? Could be days, could be weeks.

Death should be your companion in life. It shows you scarcity in time, it gives you urgency. It's a mystery but because of it we should focus in on what matters and stop wasting time on the petty. Everybody is heading to the exit. All our paths lead to the same place. Everyone should be kinder to each other.

Sunday 30th May

At 9am this morning the police knocked on my door so hard it nearly fell in. Quite the start in more ways than one. I have to admit I felt anxious as my mind tried to process every eventuality and every possible question or piece of evidence that might exist. I'm normally so good at hiding my tracks, so what was this? It was my darling they wanted, but she wasn't here. She had stayed at her house since Wednesday night and so they headed over there. That didn't give me too much confidence in their competence. They barged in on the wrong house to arrest their suspect. Idiots. I text her to say they were coming and she just replied, 'Ok x'. She didn't text again other than to say they had arrived. She was arrested. Wrongfully. I for one, know that for certain. They said they had enough evidence to suggest she was a suspect in the murder of her ex-thugfriend. When I managed to speak with her on the phone I asked what evidence, but they hadn't said. They took her, quite forcibly she said, to the station for further questioning. I hope the solicitor they provide is half decent. No real point paying for one given that I know she is completely innocent. She sounded like a frightened child. *But my darling has done nothing wrong.*

She was allowed to call me again to say she was being detained. They have said to her that they know someone was on the property just before it happened. *Well, yes.* They say is it someone he knew or trusted as there is no forced entry. *Well, yes.* But then she said, and it was quite a bombshell, that they have evidence she was in his property. *Well, absolutely no.* This is when she broke down on the phone. All I could understand was that she was sorry. She must have said it a thousand times when once would have honestly done. *Tell me what it is you need to tell me!* She said she was there. She had gone to see him, but the on the day before, on the Tuesday. She said she thought she could sort things by talking to him. So she went, *without my permission,* and they talked, and he pleaded for her to take him back. When she said no, he got angry and so she left. Did anyone see her? It would be helpful if they did. How stupid I thought, my anger felt uncontrollable, I wanted to burst but had to keep a lid on it. They haven't charged her but who else is going to be a suspect? She surely can't be convicted, she hasn't done anything and this isn't a soap opera it is real life. But then again, she has now lied twice to them, at least. About the contact on the phone and now being at his house. This is quite the mess. *You silly, silly girl.*

Monday 1st June

It's yet another Bank Holiday and no way was I going to volunteer to work this one. It is also right that the first of the month should be a Monday as then everything is in order. But Ms Hinchcliffe even tries to spoil that from beyond the grave. Lots of calls today. Apparently, my sister couldn't get hold of Ms Hinchcliffe and so phoned the police. *The police! I have had quite enough of them!* All is well though as such an old lady surely just passed away naturally.

I assume the premium bonds draw will be tomorrow and I allowed myself to think about receiving the call. It would be a double celebration if I could land the jackpot on this of all months.

My darling continues to be held but not charged. I'm sure they will let her home today. It is Bank Holiday after all. Plus, there just cannot be any actual evidence.

Tuesday 2nd June

She returned home today. When I went to pick her up, I sat waiting in the car. I didn't want to go into the police station. Sitting and waiting in a car brings about the accentuation of every creak and smell it offers. They make you fiddle with their instruments. Cars are a means of conveyance and nothing else. They are only at ease when moving. People with motor homes are mentally ill. Homes are meant to have foundations and not move. When she finally appeared, I felt relief. She looked truly terrible. As we drove home, I wondered if I'd ever see my true princess again. It felt like the woman the police took away from me had not returned and this lady who sits next to me here is a mere imposter. Has something changed inside her? Has this new and unpleasant experience left a scar, a mark that might never heal. I tried to ask how she was, but she just looked out of the window with her hands up to her chin. She was pulling at her cardigan sleeves, covering her hands as if she was still trying to hide herself and she was biting on the looser threads. It has to be said, she does look better with a bit of make-up. Not too much, but some dark mascara and a touch of lipstick does make all the difference to her appearance. She kept saying that she didn't do anything, which I, of course, *already know*. I gave her total support because I can without reservation. My total support she sees as faith but I know it as fact. I win on both counts. One thing I wasn't ready for was her questioning and reasoning as to who actually did do it. She knows she didn't, so she knows somebody else did. I hadn't reckoned on that. I said maybe it was probably just a terrible accident, like we first thought, but she said the police's line of questioning and information made that very unlikely. This is terribly inconvenient. I tried to find out what they know but I couldn't be anything other than perfectly subtle, so didn't find out anything much at all but as frustrating as that was, I will be able to chisel away at that now I have her home again.

When we got home, she said she wanted fish and chips and some dandelion and burdock. A strange request for strange times. I complied but couldn't eat mine as I felt like I was eating a warm candle with cardboard, so I made myself a chicken salad sandwich and some orange cordial. It seems that fish and chips is her meal of comfort as it takes her back to her childhood. She said she wanted to go to her house. She called it home. I said it was best for her to stay with me. She eventually agreed without saying or doing anything to really express that agreement. She wore extra bed clothes and seemed to sleep on the very edge of the bed, so I gave her space and just let her be. She has had a really tough day.

Wednesday 3rd June

Ms Hinchcliffe's funeral will be on Monday. More compassionate leave to be confirmed. It's all a game. Nobody dares question such requests. Not in these sensitive times with health and safety, compliance, equal opportunities and the like. Political correctness going mad is my friend sometimes.

I had a funny turn, or something on the way back to the train station. I came over all dizzy and felt a little weak. I had to stop, which was odd, as my usual pace is strong and quick. I'm sure it'll pass but I felt a touch worried. I don't need anything like this in my life. Maybe it was just an odd moment, a one off.

No return of texts today from my princess and when I arrived home she wasn't there. I worried for a little while and then checked the tracker I had installed on her phone. She is at her house. I have to be careful not to let her know that I can see her location at all times so I simply text 'Hello Darling, just arrived home, where have you got to x'. She replied almost instantly with 'Just at mine decorating x'. I then, inefficiently, had to be more literal in my request of her plans for the evening. She said she would eat there after she had done a bit more and that it was looking more like a home again. She said he clearly hadn't been upstairs and she was starting to feel fine about it. I could have spooked her by saying he might have, but that felt cruel just to try and make her stay with me. No need for me to join her apparently as I would only get covered in paint unnecessarily.

Nothing at all from the police today it seems. I wonder what they are up to?

Thursday 4th June

Still nothing from the police. When will they let her know she is in the clear? When can we all get back to normal? She asked me today if, for a while, she could spend some nights at her house and some at mine. This felt like something more permanent but I decided to consider it a move in the right direction, and so I said she should do whatever she is most happy with. It isn't too hard to keep spooking her about being on her own so I will drive her back into my arms and my bed before too long. *Play the long game.*

Friday 5th June

The police have said they have no further questions for her at this time but that she is still 'a person of interest', whatever that means.

They asked her not to leave the country and that if she was to go away anywhere that she should let them know. That felt so casual and so gentle I took it to be a good sign. I said it was great news and that we should celebrate but as soon as I had said it, it seemed to be an obvious miscalculation of the mood and moment. I apologised but said that I was just happy she wasn't going to have to go through any more of an ordeal. She seemed a long way from happy. She said she was tired and just wanted to go home. She called her house 'home' again and it felt like a blow. Plus, I had little chance to open up the conversation again to try and establish what they police are thinking, and what they think they know.

Saturday 6th June

I got a text from James again this morning, which seemed very, very odd. He was just, seemingly, asking how I am. I didn't feel any need to reply but something old fashioned inside always compels me to answer any question asked of me. I think that is my upbringing. I don't think younger people feel like that anymore as they can't reply to everything they see. So, I said 'fine, how are you x'. I added a kiss purely accidentally of course but men like James find this somehow hysterical and then he levered that to try and get us both to go out for a drink again. I said I'd come back to him with some dates. *I won't.*

As the evening began, I texted my darling to see if she wanted to meet up. I decided to suggest we needed to talk and maybe we could go for a bar meal. She replied 'Ok x' which gave very little away. When we met up, I used a somewhat diversionary tactic and asked her about her son. She retreated like a snail into its shell upon his very mention. Is it me or is it him? I again suggested that the three of us should meet and she said that she needed to think about it some more. She said it was a raw subject with many complications and that she needed to process her thoughts and feelings. That's what I would have said if I had wanted to swerve the idea too. I still wonder who the Dad is?

Monday 7th June

It was Ms Hinchcliffe's funeral today and it passed without incident. Nice and tidy to get it done and out of the way, plus I got to have my free day off work. There were only four of us there. Her friend, who felt obliged, my ailing sister, who looked like death itself and probably felt obliged, and me, who simply felt obliged. My darling came with me for support, so she herself also felt obliged, and she inadvertently increased the guest numbers by twenty five percent. I hadn't wanted her to come but I do want to be as close to her as possible so I relented in the knowledge that there could be very little harm done and there might be something to gain for me, for us. We might bond together in grief somehow. She might feel something for me in this false plight of mine. Somehow, I didn't like it when my darling spoke to my sister. I just hadn't considered the idea. I just didn't like two separate worlds engaging in that way. They seemed to be talking whenever I was out of earshot and as they spoke, they kept glancing at me.

The weather was pleasant so you might have thought more would turn out. Surely someone, anyone else might have attended? I'll have to pretend to be surprised when her will is read in the coming days. She was nothing to nobody and I could see why.

Tuesday 8th June

Nothing from the police again today and whilst silence is golden, I do wonder what they are thinking and doing and whether they are making any ground? Hopefully they are simply giving up and putting it down as an accident. I am sure they have better things to do. This whole thing is more than inconvenient and it is affecting my precious sleep. Why couldn't they have just accepted it was an accident in the first place? What will they do with my darling? Will she ever feel free of them? *Well of course yes, as she is innocent.* I think it will all just blow over and eventually they will give up. They don't seem to have any hard evidence whatsoever, just the stories they are telling themselves. It's not as if I can do anything to find out and why would I want to poke that particular wasps nest anyway? That would only bring a spotlight on me. I wish she would open up and talk to me about it, the longer she doesn't, the more she will forget about what was said. Her memory isn't the best.

Wednesday 9th June

Work is such a drag at the moment. I've been to more strategy sessions than actual work meetings recently. I am sure there are some really good consultants out there, but this lot are salesmen selling hot air and my company is buying. They love to just hypothesize. Did any of them ever earn a proper living doing an actual job. Ever?

Still, it is not too long until I can realise my dream and pack this all in. I allowed myself, mid strategy meeting, to dream of our cottage in the South West and it made me smile. I was brought back to earth when I was asked a direct question. I felt like a naughty schoolboy. I had no idea of the question, so I said, 'Well, that is indeed interesting. I'd need to think about it and come back to you'. I have absolutely no idea, even now, if that was an appropriate response. And, to be frank, I didn't much care.

Thursday 10th June

People always ask 'How are you?' but it's not a real question, more a greeting. They don't really want to know how you are. They don't really want to know about my piles, my neurosis or my continual disappointment with daily life. What a shock it would be if we all started to answer this literally. It would take forever and so they would just change the question to something else.

Friday 11th June

I tried to plan something nice for us both this evening but my darling is still not anything like her usual self. I cooked us a lovely meal but she seemed to just push it around the plate. She does seem to have become thinner and she really doesn't need to, as she is perfect just the way she was. I feel like she is trying to avoid staying over at my house, with me.

Saturday 12th June

Another text from James this morning asking if I am free this evening. Just go away. I text back to say, 'I am very expensive' and my terrible joke was ill thought through as it just encouraged him to engage more. Why can't he get it through his thick head that I don't want anything more to do with him. He is like a barnacle on a ship, just too hard to shake off. I ended up saying 'maybe in the week' to end the exchange and give him nothing too specific to cling to.

I didn't see my darling today as she said she felt ill and had a headache. Another excuse? I said I could go round and care for her but she gave me the brush off. I told her to rest and make sure she eats and drinks properly and she just replied with one kiss. That really seemed to end our communication in its tracks. *She is all alone, she only has me, but she won't let me care for her.*

Sunday 13th June

I woke up really late this morning and it took a while for me to pull away from a lovely deep sleep. A large part of me didn't want to. For once I decided to just lie there and contemplate for a while. I didn't really kick start for a little while and my sleep-soaked brain actually felt like a friend for a change. My half trance was broken by a text, which annoyed me until I realised it was from her. She says she is feeling a little better and she suggests a walk later on. Yes, dear, of course, whatever you wish.

The walk was lovely but relations are strained. She isn't opening up to me and I therefore cannot see the full flower of her inner beauty. I was as kind and gentle as can be and sometimes I saw a glimmer of what I craved, even if it was just a half smile. We walked and talked and eventually we got a coffee and sat outside in the evening sun. I really wanted to probe into her time with the police but it just felt like the wrong moment. There was no way into this fragile state without bulldozing in and breaking something on the way. So, I tried just asking her to open up about anything she felt like saying. She talked about her son for a bit, but no invite for me. She talked about missing work a bit, but that she didn't want to go back. She spoke about her ex-boyfriend and how she could never wish anyone any harm, she said she just wanted him to leave her alone and now the police think she is a murderer. *There we are, I thought, here I go.* But she couldn't stop herself from crying. She couldn't string two words together and people started to look. So, I just moved round and comforted her. I held her and told her everything was going to be okay. That's what people say to each other in that situation.

Monday 14th June

The last will and testament was read today but I didn't even go. I left it to my sister to tell me what I already knew. I acted mildly surprised but couldn't rouse myself to fully act my part out. The actor must always, at least, find his motivation. I said that she should have enough now to pay for her medical bills, but she said that it was too late now and the course was set. Really? I thought. Sounds to me like you'd rather keep the money for something else, but you were very happy to spend mine. Says it all and made me feel surer of my decision. I do hope that if the disease kills my sister, then that might mean I finally get my rightful share. *So, play nice.*

Tuesday 15th June

Work kept me mildly busy today, but I found myself and my thoughts just wandering around and considering many things. Firstly, my sister and how any small feelings I have for her are quite negative. Secondly, my princess and how we must not let anything change our course and thirdly, my parents. What a hand I have been dealt. *And how I have played it.*

Wednesday 16th June

Works acts as a distraction in life. It offers us some sort of zombie state to help us get through the day. It gets you up early, it makes you spend time travelling, it dulls your brain as you work hard and long for someone or something else and it tires you out so that you have nothing left but the need for food and sleep. You are made to believe you are on a journey to somewhere. *But are we?*

Thursday 17th June

The local paper decided to cover the house fire as its lead story this week. The headline read 'House inferno' which was hardly inventive or helpful. Apparently, if you bought a copy you could read the 'full, inside story'. I bought a copy to see what might be said by the police, but it was utter dross and of no use at all. There was an appeal for more information and a hotline, loads of pictures of the house burnt to a crisp with fire engines in view and lots of 'No comment' from the police. A slow news week I imagine and as soon as these rags are wrapping fish and chips the better. They still make your fingers all black and dirty. Do newspapers in their physical form have any use nowadays? I have absolutely no barometer of local gossip so I stupidly tried to kill two birds with one stone and invited James out for a drink. He seemed delighted. I ultimately killed neither bird nor had a stone. I had to start with an apology for my earlier harsh behaviour, but this only seemed to bring out the brash and stupid side of him, like it had given him an upper hand of sorts. My idea was to assess local mood, local gossip and interest but all I got was an earful of misogyny and a face covered with saliva due to his disgusting habit of spitting whilst talking. I tried talking to the bar staff when he went to the toilet, which seemed to be quite frequently, but they all seemingly had absolutely zero interest in the local paper that sat on the bar. Most of them hadn't even seen the story or heard of it. I stopped asking quite quickly as I didn't want to seem too interested. I waited until he had drunk just enough to be the wrong side of sober and I left without a goodbye. He is an oxygen thief.

Friday 18th June

So many lies are told everyday by, seemingly, everyone. But sometimes it is possible to be perfectly truthful and yet mistaken and that is quite a different thing. There's something about ones intent. We each know deep down, and we each justify our actions to ourselves. I doubt anyone has or could live their whole life being truly, fully honest. That feels somehow disappointing and sad, yet very real. *Does it really matter?* How would such a person, a totally, truly honest person fare in life? Would they be better off or worse off? I am not going to be the guinea pig to find out, that is for sure. Sometimes there is no actual lie, but you mislead on purpose. You skew the facts to your benefit. *Is that actually lying?* Is that better or worse? To simply use facts to your advantage. Do lies always do harm or are they sometimes justified? There are many examples of where I feel it is better to lie. What about tact? Lies are given such a bad name but what about the good things we fail to do, the things we decide not to do? Surely, they are of the same result and consequence and are just as bad as lying?. As long as the other person thinks you are telling the truth, you are safe, but what about liars' guilt? Can we reconcile ourselves to our lies, can we justify these things internally or do they chip away at your integrity and your soul over time? Is there a reckoning day? Religion would have you believe that there is but that may well be a lie itself. Ultimately, is it truly possible to lie to yourself? What do we each actually believe, and have we been able to lie to ourselves and, if so, how would we even know? It has become so commonplace and normal, nobody knows where the lines are anymore.

Saturday 19th June

The weekend brings rest but also it allows your brain to scan and offer you no respite. It sees the gap in the week as its chance to remind you of all you might worry about. It seeks, it finds and it reports back. It is trying to protect you but, at times, it really does overdo it.

Sunday 20th June

I woke up thinking that the leap year curse may have lifted this year as nothing bad has happened, only good. I have my darling at my side, of sorts, and I have a plan to leave the rat race and I have a future where my darling and I will live happily and simply by the sea and in the warm. We just need a few loose ends to tie up and this could well be the happiest year of my, of our, lives.

Monday 21st June

Is today the longest day of the year? Well, it certainly felt so. Nothing good happened. James text me to say nothing. Clearly, he felt aggrieved at me just leaving him on Thursday whereas he should be more embarrassed about how he chooses to behave. My darling seems too distant, and I cannot yet assess how much is coming to me from Ms Hinchcliffe. Although I know it's less than I am rightfully due, by percentage. I had no reason to reach out and talk to anyone today. I felt listless and I felt like I spent most of the day just looking out of the window. It felt, to me, like everyone at work was playing the same game, just letting the hours of our lives drift by, letting the working day float through us with the promise of a gentle summer evening. If you steal time at work and are getting paid for doing nothing on purpose, is that as bad as say, stealing a stapler? Even the bus and the train seemed quieter and slower than usual.

When I eventually went to bed, I tried to count just how many people I had spoken to all day. I think it was four.

Tuesday 22nd June

Another thrilling day at work. The sort of day that makes you try and count how many you have left.

The most important part of the day was the evening. I was visited by the police who wanted to 'establish some facts'. They asked me about my movements on the day of the fire. I was at work officer. And they probed about my darling. Like a skilled tightrope walker, I gave them just enough to make sure she was still the prime suspect. Just enough doubt cast and I ensured that I looked like I was trying to protect her and certainly I gave enough for them to in no way consider me. *Oh, I can really act. I was so very helpful. If you need anything else, then just please do ask.*

Wednesday 23rd June

Peaceful, honest people have the right to be left alone. So just leave me alone.

We will all be dead soon enough, so why do we focus on the petty so much? Time is both free and priceless.

Thursday 24th June

I awoke in the middle of the night. My mother is gone and I appear to be the end of the family line. My sister is hardly going to step up to the plate now is she. Do I have any kind of responsibility? Is there something I should be doing? Like having children? Maybe I should propose to my darling and we should both consider this? *Children!*

Friday 25th June

It was one of those national charity days today. Those days where everyone becomes really annoying and people try to draw attention to themselves whilst trying to convince you they are doing it for charity and not for their own ego and self-promotion. There was a clown on the bus. This false humility of *'don't look at me, this is really uncomfortable, I know I look stupid but it's for a great cause, I am doing this for children around the world'* when it's really *'look at me, look how great I am, don't stop, look at me, me, me'*.

Tonight's television will be bombarded with multi-millionaire celebrities looking down the camera at working class people, begging them to donate a pound whilst pounding them with the telephone number to do it on. There real focus is furthering their own careers and looking magnanimous. Perhaps they even believe they are good souls. I can't take anymore of those patronising clips and those same whiny singers playing their latest, awful song.

Saturday 26th June

Lots of loose ends for a Saturday. What are the police doing? More importantly, what are they thinking and how can I find out? What is my darling thinking and when will she be ready for us to be back together properly? Can I really propose? Can I and will I really hand my notice in when my shares are mine fully? What is happening with Ms Hinchcliffes will? What will I get, when will I know, how long will it take to sell her property?

I felt my mind racing. I was irritable. I tried to text my darling but couldn't quite find the right words so just kept deleting the words before anything was sent. I noticed only too well that she didn't text me. I couldn't even settle to make myself some nice food. The television just annoyed me and the radio wasn't enough. Even a trusty long walk felt wrong. My mood the whole day was like the not so calm before the oncoming inevitable storm.

Sunday 27th June

Remarkably, I slept well. I managed to watch some drippy comedy before sleep and somehow my brain was fooled. I woke up in a much more melancholy frame of mind than I deserved. Whilst my brain was fooled, I tried to take advantage and text my princess. I said I needed somebody with everything that was going on. I said I just wanted to talk, to clear my head and that she is the only one I could ever really open up to. My texts, whilst numerous, were compelling and impossible to ignore. I had hit the bullseye and within a few minutes she had replied to say that she had been up for a while already and why didn't we go for a walk and have a chat. *It's a start.*

I was so humble, so generous and unassuming. I tried to be the person she fell for in the first place. I was careful with humour though I knew it had a role to play. I've always been able to make her laugh. I took nothing for granted. I expressed myself openly. I talked, *lied*, about Ms Hinchcliffe and I broke my golden rule and referred to her as my mother. *Needs must.* This was when my hooks sank in the deepest. She said she really understood, she really felt my pain. I looked all sad eyed at her, clearly craving a hug whilst always giving the impression that I didn't deserve or expect one. When she was warmed up, I asked her if the police had been in touch. I wanted to gain information without imparting any and I noticed a subtle change, a hardening of her lips. *She has been told not to discuss this, but by who and why?* I realised I had nothing to gain there but something to lose so I turned the conversation back and spoke about my sister. I said I was burdened with irremovable guilt. *I really am not.* I said that I felt she had cornered me into an impossible position and that I felt truly awful. She seemed to believe me and she sided with me and said she understood. I asked about her son and asked if they were getting closer. The lips tightened again, so I had to reverse. Finally, and perhaps somewhat desperately I asked her, pleaded with her really, to take a step towards me, to come back in my direction and to give us the chance to reconcile, to heal. I explained how she had changed my life, how she was so good for me and how we are great together. I felt like she was swaying, literally swaying on her feet as an indication of what the different forces of her mind were telling her to do. I had to push but not over push. I gave it everything I had. I moved towards her and gave her a hug. She half hugged me back and then she needed time to think and that she had to go. I said I completely understood. I stood, faux frozen to the spot. All I wanted was for her to half look back as she walked away. I knew how crucial it was that she did and just when I had given up, just at the end of the reaches of our natural vision, she half stopped and looked back at me over my shoulder. A day of significant progress. I went home happy. *Everything will come together.*

Monday 28th June

Thankfully Ms Hinchcliffe appointed her solicitor as executor of her will. Whilst this means a slightly smaller cut for me, due to the fees these greedy pigs take, it will save me any hassle. A windfall beckons once everything is sold. My sister text me to ask if there were any personal items that I wanted from her house. I didn't dare text back 'the iPad'. There isn't anything, but I tried to remember if she had any expensive jewellery as I could then pretend it meant something to me and then I could sell it. I said I'd have a think. I'd have to be specific for it to work. Maybe I could try for a ring and then use it to propose, pass on a family heirloom, give it some real meaning and save probably around a thousand pounds or more. I should have paid more attention to the detail, I'd need to be specific. I'm annoyed at myself for that. There must be something I can pine for, *something that meant the world to me.*

In the end I just said I wanted my half.

Tuesday 29th June

I used the will as a lever to get back in touch. I used a teasing text to say I had the details of my mother's will *(Ms Hinchcliffe's)*, and that I could really use a chat. Rather coldly she told me to call her after work.

The call did not work as I had hoped. She seemed cold and somewhat distant. If I didn't know better, I'd say she was trying to watch television or read a book at the same time. It was only afterwards that I wondered who she has in her ear, whether someone was undoing all my good work in the meantime. I'm creating, knitting, only for someone to pull away at the threads when I am not there. This is something I need to deal with, but my foe, for now, is invisible to me.

Wednesday 30th June

It is share option day tomorrow. I tried to create an inner excitement about it but it just didn't work. It's just admin really and the real celebration will be when the shares are fully mine and my resignation is in place. Then I'll be able to surprise my darling and pull her closer, bring her back to me and we will be able to start to plan and execute our new lives together, way away from here. All baggage left behind. Now that did put a spring in my step and bring a smile to my lips.

Thursday 1st July

Finally, my share option matured today so now I fully and unequivocally own the shares. They are all mine and I don't need to work here a day longer. But I will do exactly that. I will work here one day longer. Actually, I plan to give my notice in tomorrow, but I hope they will let me go almost instantly to allow my freedom to begin without delay. I've worked out my financial situation on a spreadsheet and as long as I am dutiful and careful, I have enough to see me through without having to work. I might well get a job, maybe local, maybe part-time, just to give myself something to do and a few more pennies to spend, but I don't have to if I don't want to. This will all be a terrific surprise for my darling. I am starting to wonder more and more about our future though. I can no longer be sure whether she will love that we can spend so much more time together. What a surprise I have made for her but will it now all fall flat. It must not. We really can go and buy our cottage and just be together without all these distractions and all this nonsense around us. *When it is just us two again, it will be magical, just like before.*

Friday 2nd July

I actually did it, I handed in my resignation after all these years. There was a touch of shock from one or two but basically nothing. My boss said it would be processed and then I would receive a formal letter via email. I'm not quite sure what I expected but I was certainly a touch underwhelmed on all counts. I felt like I somehow deserved more, but maybe that's just ego?

News travelled fast though as chief rat, or the senior consultant as I think he prefers to be called, came over and said, 'So you are leaving?' which was about the most pointless thing anyone has ever said to me. I said it was confidential just to spook him a little. He wanted to know where I was going. Such an assumption. I said I'd rather not say. And then the greasy rat asked if I would like some of his business cards to take with me to his new place. I said, 'Yes, sure, then I can make it really clear just who they should be avoiding and by what distance'. Idiot.

I get to surprise my darling tonight with our new life. I am, perhaps, a touch nervous. I think maybe I'll save the news until tomorrow and then I can pick my moment. I cannot wait. We'll have everything we need. We will be away from all of this. *Just her and me.* We will leave our history behind us.

Saturday 3rd July

I waited as long as I physically could. I didn't see her until the evening. I managed to persuade her to come round on a mini false pretence and then I told my darling my news. But then she told me hers. After insisting I go first, I ended up feeling like an idiot. It all turned out more than a bit flat and miscalculated. I was angry and confused. Just as I explained what I had done all she could ask is whether I have the right to rescind my resignation. It turns out I do, but there is no way back, not morally nor with any chance of keeping my pride in place. I explained about the share option, about freedom, even about maybe buying our cottage in Devon or Cornwall. That's when she stopped me and pulled exactly the wrong face. She had assumed that I had assumed that she was looking for a new job. That's how she told it anyway. As fate would have it, she accepted her new job on the very same day I resigned from mine, and she starts on the 1st August. I felt numb, I felt silly and only then did I feel the rage. She just hadn't thought things through. She hadn't told me she needed to go back to work, that she wanted to go back to work. I rushed my food, had nothing to say and we parted and she went back to that place she now always seem to refer to as 'home'. I am confused, angry and ready to do....I *don't know quite what.* I am betrayed. Never mind if I can rescind my resignation, can she turn this job offer down before it is too late. I can work on that.

Sunday 4th July

It's not that she cannot turn the job offer down it is that she *actually doesn't want to.* She says she misses the 'meaning and purpose' work gives, she misses the difficulty and the sense of achievement, she misses the Monday morning dread and the Friday evening delight, and she misses the feeling of validation and self-esteem that pay day brings. She misses the camaraderie. Her whole soliloquy was both compelling and disgusting. The hamster wants to get back on the wheel. *Open your eyes woman.* I still have some time, but I must work at this well. It's a big job.

Monday 5th July

I couldn't sleep last night. I just didn't feel right with myself. When I woke up, I was lightheaded and a little dizzy and felt very strange. I might go and see the doctor. I feel like this happens now and again and more often.

Work have told me I must serve a full one months' notice. Fine I said. One month is nothing after all these years. I will hardly be lifting a finger anyway. But they have now inadvertently insisted that I cannot be with my darling, even for this one month. So I must, I simply must sabotage her new job. There must be a way to do this with her full blessing. I must be able to win her over.

Tuesday 6th July

I text her this morning. I said 'I come in peace x'. I said I wanted to talk. I said that things had been really stressful for us both recently and that we needed a 'reset'. I told her I loved her and that all I wanted is the best future together we could carve and that all I really wanted to do was to make her as happy as possible. I felt like people were watching me text. Nosey parkers. I had, somewhat inadvertently, text her seven times before I realised that she hadn't replied.

Work have already worked out how to replace me and to fill the gap I am going to leave. I have to train various people up on the various tasks I undertake. They genuinely show no interest in what I was telling them. I urge them to pay attention and take some notes but I soon give up caring as well. It is not going to be my problem come August but I will have some bigger issues if she doesn't turn down that job soon. If she doesn't, I'll have to come up with a 'plan b'. I'd rather do it the easy way, with her onside.

On the way home I text her again. Nothing from her at all today. I felt like she was being rude and disrespectful given my olive branch in the morning. I need to see her. How can I sort this out with her if we don't meet or even talk?

Wednesday 7th July

I went for a walk today to try and clear my head. Everyone in a vehicle seems to either be on the phone or listening to music and whichever one it is they do it far too loudly. You can hear every syllable of their meaningless, empty conversation yet, somehow it seems to give them a hugely inflated sense of importance. The technology is surely normal enough for us now to see its novelty value reduce. *Not for some it seems.* Whenever these vehicles have the radio on, all of the DJ's sound the same. They sound happy but not in an authentic way. They all have these half American accents and sound like they have just been released from the asylum with a little too much medication flowing through their veins. If you ever actually hear a song playing it's the same voice, the same noise. Please stop trying to manufacture a song that everybody will like and try making a song that *you* really like. Yes, I do feel old today.

Thursday 8th July

Finally, she agreed for us to meet, but again whilst walking. The weather was glorious and on my way there I hoped that it would help lift our spirits and see possibilities. I decided to open up, to tell her how much I wanted to sort things out fully with her and my dream of us being together and I subtly suggested just how her new job would get in the way of that. She said she was still shaken by recent events, by the fire and therefore she needed more time. She also said she wanted to ensure she had financial independence and just how important that was to her. It may have been the sun and it may have been a bit desperate but my best attempt to win her back was to propose marriage. I said it was all I had ever wanted. *I don't even want to get married, I didn't even have a ring!* I said it would complete our lives and it would give her all the independence and security she could ever need. It, somehow, felt like a less than gentle plea. I knew my offer was reversible in time, but I also knew it would entwine us together in her eyes irrevocably and offer me the chance of having her as mine again, fully. I stood there, she stood there. We looked each other in the eye. I was sure a 'yes' was arriving on her lips but then she just let out an odd yelp and she ran. I was frozen to the spot. I couldn't see anything or anyone else, just her running away as fast as she could with her hand over her mouth.

Friday 9th July

She text me first this morning to tell me she hadn't slept and that she needed time to think and not to contact her for a little while. I took this as a bad sign. But my journey in to work also allowed me to plan my anonymous call to her new employer. I'll make the call next week if she hasn't said yes to me by then and I'll make sure they are indeed, not, her new employer.

Saturday 10th July

I awoke again in the early hours. In the middle of the night even small things seem impossible. I thought about the lesser things I needed to do and they felt huge. I thought about the past, my brain scanning for problems, regrets and then future anxieties. I knew that as the light seeped in through the gap in the curtains it would bring with it a new bravery and gusto but at that moment I felt daunted, like a small child, about just facing the day.

I feel back asleep but was then rudely awoken by a knock at the door. These largely unwelcome visitors are like constant invaders and the front door is the barrier they must face yet they use it as their calling signal. You cannot, somehow, simply ignore them. They each come to your door for them, not for you. *Buy this, listen to this, do this, give me this.* Even the delivery drivers, who now dominate suburbia with their white transit vans, bang, knock and holler as if they are judge, jury and king. Somehow you owe them for the huge favour they are doing you. These visitors pinch your time unforgivingly, unapologetically and somehow the burden is then on you to shoo them away, you assume responsibility even though it was them that invaded your space. Today's knocker and doorbell ignorer was a young chap who said he is trying to make his way after some time in prison. He was selling tat from a holdall. A fiver for three dusters and I ended up buying said dusters due to his mild, possibly unintentional intimidation and the size of his biceps. A fiver for him to like me and not to think of coming back and harming me and my house felt like a good deal. It was as close as I have ever come to being in an episode of The Sopranos. The irony that I only bought them because of his history and not due to his attempts to leave that behind was likely lost on him. Some sales pitch though, I thought.

Sunday 11th July

I felt at a loose end today. I started a few things but couldn't settle to anything. In the end I just sat in the garden and enjoyed the sunshine. I looked at my phone in the vain hope she would text. I even considered texting James but quickly came to my senses. I wondered, in the early evening if I enjoyed my solitude today or whether I felt a bit lonely. I never once considered contacting my sister.

I do need to know what she is thinking. How can she stay silent and distant given what I have just asked of her?

Monday 12th July

If she doesn't text me, I will make the phone call tomorrow. Enough is enough. I had written the details down on a piece of paper that I can later shred and I'd pop out at lunchtime and use a payphone. I had looked around for one on recent lunchtime walks and realised there are so very few of them anymore, which makes sense as I haven't used one myself in years. I did find a suitable one. It felt right.

In the afternoon we all received an email advising us of an outward bound course in August. A team building and trust building exercise, it explained. Every employee must attend, unless you can prove medical exemption. I heard the slow audible sigh rise up through the office as the emails pinged and were opened. I saw people have those little across desk conversations as they tried to process the news and thought about all their own foibles and fears. It was with great joy that I knew I would have left this place by then but they were too lazy to exclude me from the email group and so I had the joy of pouring over the details in the knowledge that I wouldn't have to attend. How splendid. I said it was a huge shame that I couldn't join them and how much I would have loved to. Every single one of them appreciated the sarcasm. They were all assessing which groups and dates they had been given and it was quickly clear that a conscious effort had been made to keep 'friends' apart. I laughed inside at it all. Strangely though, at some point on the bus journey home, I then imagined them all getting on with it and being together and laughing and getting paid to mess around. I imagined the fun I could have had just gently teasing and making fun. I couldn't believe I felt this way. I got on the bus happy and with a spring in my step and I got off the bus a little sad and dejected. That is the wrong way round for the bus home.

Tuesday 13th July

Still nothing from her so she has forced me into action. A 'yes' does not take this long. I hadn't considered, until I dialled the number, that I might have to conceal my voice. I decided to go lower and try a Scottish accent. Everyone trusts a Scotsman and I can really act, in fact I often wish I'd tried my hand at acting earlier in life and maybe it's still not too late. I got through to a lovely lady in HR and explained that my precious darling was unfit for the role and gave a variety of compelling reasons why, including her recent arrest for the murder of her ex-boyfriend. I was plausible, I think. I'd thought it through and, of course, was only acting in the interests of their company and its reputation.

On the way home I wondered if that now meant there was no way back for us as a couple but then I reminded myself, with a smile, nay a chuckle, that, of course, she has no knowledge whatsoever about what I have done. So actually, if she accepts my proposal, everything could work out perfectly and we might yet get our cottage, just the two of us, eventually, after all.

Wednesday 14th July

The thought occurred to me this morning that I might need to better plan my leaving work. I can't quite call it retirement somehow. It feels more like an escape and my picture of a retired person is much older than I am. Of course, I did have it all planned out, she was supposed to be with me and we were supposed to be exploring a new life with all of our baggage left behind. How can I convince her she doesn't need this new job, that she will be happier without it? Maybe a change of tack is needed and maybe my call will work. I'll work all angles to get what I want, what she really needs.

I wonder how I will find out about the result of my call! I can hardly ask her. My only chance to sort this properly is by getting into my darling's head. But to do that, we must be talking, properly, with full trust and love.

Thursday 15th July

Work is a real drag at the moment. I don't care, they don't care and the people I'm meant to be training up don't care. I get the feeling my perfectly efficient and well-run systems will not be in anyway suitably maintained. I really thought they were precious to me and I thought the company valued what I did. Both seem to be untrue. I haven't had any moments or conversations to mark my departure and I really doubt I will keep in touch with anyone at all. It really does go to show that all that effort, all that stress we feel and the amount we care is just a total waste of our heart and our mind.

Friday 16th July

I'm counting the days down now and have started to use my work calendar in the manner of an escaping prisoner. I've made sure this is noticeable to passers-by of my desk. Big red and black crosses marking the days off as I go. I had a lovely walk at lunchtime and for the first time in my life I was late back. I felt a panic, a stress about that. Oh, how conditioned we become by work norms and by our own habits. I just sat back at my desk a full six minutes late from lunch and nobody said or did anything. Nobody cared one jot.

Now the weekend is approaching I considered whether my darling has had enough time yet? It is a full calendar week now. Can we talk? I spent a large part of my afternoon composing a text in my mind to do the job as effectively as possible. I went with, 'I'm not trying to disturb your solitude but could we maybe talk, or meet this weekend? I miss you terribly and only want to ensure you are happy x'. To be honest, I'm not sure it is my best effort but she can't control the timeline forever. *She has had long enough.*

I got a reply on my journey home. She knew I'd be travelling at that time. 'Let's talk tomorrow x' she said. No details, no confirmation of the medium we are to employ or the timing. Vague, but not without hope.

Saturday 17th July

I had a lovely deep sleep overnight. These things can feel random at times. Why such a good sleep last night I thought? Is the best part of the day the bit just as you fall asleep, the minute or so when you wake up, before your brain and all its realities kick in, or maybe the time you are actually asleep in itself? This comforts me that death will bring no hurdles, no pain, as I regard it as the brother of sleep in many ways.

I waited. I wanted to text but I waited. *Let her think this is on her terms.* And eventually, after midday, a text. Unexpected but then so predictable. 'Let's meet in the park at 2.30, is that ok? x'. I'd prefer we were more private. At my house. There is more to work with here. My last vision of us at the park is her running off, looking like she is going to be sick, *sick at my marriage proposal.* I'll put that out of my mind and consider this the first step back. I need her to want to be with me again, I need her to pack in this job before it starts but I have come to realise exactly where we are and that I must take small steps. Any step in the right direction is a good one. Success at any speed.

Sunday 18th July

So, we chatted all evening, we watched the sun come down over the duck pond. There were encouraging flashes of vulnerability. On occasion, it felt like old times. But I did sense a new, hardened resolve against me as well. Is somebody in her ear? Who? I chipped away at her with all the subtlety I could muster. I tried to be all the things I thought she liked in me. I tried to be gentle, funny, loving and caring. I was apologetic. I explained just how much I missed her. I brought up old private jokes and little shared moments. I explained how much respect I had for her and her individuality and her right to make all her own choices. I told her I would like to start again, almost. I said I would like us to try to build a path together, brick by brick and that we are much better together than apart. I told her my proposal was heartfelt and that I meant it but that it was more important to me that she was totally comfortable with herself and that she could say 'no' and that I would respect that. I told her that we had time but that we could still, eventually, fulfil our dream of a new home in the South West, by the coast. I said the way back is through talking, through deepening our understanding and recapturing our love. I think I sowed enough seeds, I think I worked my way inside her. I suggested I could cook a special meal for us both tomorrow, or whenever suited her and whilst I could feel her resistance she finally relented. So, she is coming over for tea tomorrow evening. When she arrives, I will be behind with the cooking to make her stay longer. I'll have all the right homely smells, I'll make sure her part of my garden looks in need of attention. I look just a bit of a mess to bring out her maternal, caring instincts. I'll look strong but vulnerable, together yet alone.

I really, *really*, should have been an actor.

Monday 19th July

Only one more Monday after this one to make this two-legged commute. Four legs a day in total. I wanted to tell all of these familiar faces about my escape but, whilst they are familiar to me, I know nothing of them as people. I could accurately draw their haunted faces from memory but I don't know any of their names. The only time we've ever spoken, or grunted, to be more accurate, is when we have to do seat shuffling, let people in, or ask the selfish ones to take their bags of spare seats. What is it about human nature that means we don't talk to each other? If we worked together, or even met at a party, we would say hello and chat and we would then, hopefully, find one or two we might like or have something in common with, but on public transport, this is somehow forbidden, it is an absolute non-starter. *How very strange.*

Our evening get together went like a dream. She melted in front of me. She saw all the good in me, all the things we had in the first place. She was the audience to my play. My prey. I didn't mention her new job, not once. I couldn't, tactically. I was aching for her to raise it and say she had decided not to proceed. I had even practised my shocked face in case she said they had withdrawn their offer and not explained why. *I wish.* But nothing, no mention. There is still time though.

I decided to follow up with a text before bed and said maybe we could meet for a walk to continue the conversation. She said she would meet me for lunch tomorrow. That came as a bit of surprise to be honest. Even later on she text to say she was going to pop into the office to say hello to some of her old colleagues and friends. *How brave, how unexpected.* This came across as somewhat audacious, almost brazen. Where is this new confidence coming from and why does she want to do that? I have no choice but to go along with it. It might not be perfect, but it is progress.

Tuesday 20th July

She strolled into the office with unnerving confidence. Almost like she owned the place, a queen back in her palace. I observed her closely whilst, for my benefit and that of colleagues, I tried not to look overly interested. She seemed fleeting with the people I thought she was closest to and then seemed to spend too much time with a couple of the chaps in IT. She didn't used to engage with them all that much when she worked here so why today? Was there a purpose? I walked over that way as casually as I could but when I got within earshot they seemed to stop talking. I then said 'Hi' as if her visit was a surprise and I suggested a lunchtime walk as if it were an 'off the hoof' idea. She looked at me in a new way. *Like I was an idiot.* Clearly, I instantly realised that she must have told others we had pre-arranged the walk but how was I to know that? I did, therefore, indeed look like an idiot but it was the look she gave me that I didn't appreciate. The power she exhibited, the authority. You are not in charge, my love. I was made to feel, fleetingly, like the sub-ordinate, the child. I cannot have her confidence reaching such levels, but I must bide my time and make light of the whole thing. I must gently apologise and admit my idiocy as I plot the path back to where I need her to be. Plus, hopefully her visit to the office will remind her that the work environment is not something she really wishes to re-enter.

It is later and as I lie in bed, I write this to try and clear my head and organise my thoughts. I just can't get over her just strolling into the office, just talking to people she barely knows. Also just saying 'hi' to people who joined after she left. Literally, just introducing herself. She looked so confident, so appealing and so gorgeous. Did she say that she is still with me? Did people ask? How big of an idiot did I look saying 'Hey, let's go for a walk!' when she had undoubtedly already told everyone that's why she was here. And the walk itself. Her stride was so assured, her attitude so impregnable. There were just a few occasions where she looked a little nervous, but to the untrained eye they were barely detectable. Have I lost control of this at this moment in time? I had no option but to stay on course, to apologise and make light of my faux pas. To compliment her on everything from her attitude, her inner beauty and her confidence. I tried to anchor and link the visit to when we met in an attempt to stir up the initial feelings she had for me. Those feelings at the beginning of a relationship are never beaten, so to stir them to the surface can only help. She seemed to slow time me though. More control for her as she knew I was against the clock, and she wasn't. No commitment from her and still no mention of the job. Not even a proper reply to my proposal. I feel impotent, like a poker player whose cards are face up on the table, revealed with nothing further to play, only the option of waiting to see what the other player has. To see if I have won or lost. And that is where I am. I am at the mercy of her next actions, and I do not know what they will be. I did not sleep well.

Wednesday 21st July

It's mid-summer and the weather seemed to know as today was the hottest day of the year so far. At work, the idea of a summer ball was mentioned and the CEO agreed it was a good idea for staff morale but said he didn't want the company to organise it. He said he would 'throw some money at the bar'. The English language is dying in front of us and its replacement is far worse. Every word now has to be of the highest impact and most dramatic meaning which then means there is no impact and drama at all as that is the point of language in the first place. There are enough words to articulate things as they need to be. One of the consultants brought another a cup of water on the hottest day of the year and the recipient described this act of walking three yards to get two cups of water instead of one as 'Awesome'. So, I searched 'Awesome' and it means 'extremely impressive or daunting; inspiring awe. The awesome power of the atomic bomb'. I mean is one additional, small cup of water carried indoors over a small distance for a colleague really 'Awesome'. I would say not.

Nothing from my darling today. I cannot stand her games. I cannot stand them. Maybe it is just the heat getting to me.

After work, I sat in the garden with a cool long drink. I took my shoes and socks off and put my feet on the grass. I loved feeling connected to nature but then my mind, as ever, presented the possibility of something crawling up my leg or biting me or living in my skin undetected for years. Leave me alone I thought, as I put my socks back on.

Thursday 22nd July

I couldn't help but text her this morning. Surely, she has something to say by now. I simply said 'Hello, how are you. I miss you, can we talk x'. I expected another invitation to the park but even that mild expectation wasn't met as I simply received no reply. I tried not to look at my phone, but I must have looked at it over a thousand times in the end. I've turned off all notifications and beeps as they grate too much. They are so invasive, so immediate in their need for a view or a response. I even feel irritated by other people's pings, bings, rings and alerts. The worst ones are those neanderthals who insist on having really loud music when somebody calls them. They want everyone within a half mile to know somebody has rung them and then they continue their charade by speaking just as loudly as their ringtone. It's hard to ignore. They smile at the end with satisfaction, as if they have achieved a goal of seeming important.

This thought must have stayed with me as when I got home and watched some television as I noticed, and seemed perhaps overly sensitive to, the adverts being louder than the programmes. I thank god, any of the gods, for the mute button.

And still no reply from her. How could she not have seen my text? I might go round tomorrow. Should I go announced or should it be a surprise visit? Well, I'll text again and if no reply, I will surprise her. I'll take her a gift.

Friday 23rd July

I decided not to text her again and just wait for the reply I felt I was owed. That is me, trying to play it cool. Which is not really me at all and is harder than usual given the heatwave we now appear to be in. I listened to the weather forecast this morning but of course no specifics, just very enthusiastic generalisations for someone hedging their bets and looking, no doubt, to further their own career and cause. I mean, 'hot in the north' is about as useless a piece of information as you could get. They might as well say, 'look out of the window'. I'm trying to work out whether to water my grass. It's turning brown in its appeal to for a drink. I'll hang on a while, maybe, as it is durable stuff. The other year my neighbour got a fine for watering her grass and washing her car in the middle of a heatwave. Or so I heard.

During the afternoon I eventually got a text back from her which annoyed me as it wrestled the possibility of a surprise visit away from me. It said 'Sorry, been busy and been thinking. Yes, let's talk, when are you free this weekend'. I noted the lack of a kiss. I noted the cold calculation and the non-specific arrangement with many options to get out and delay. Maybe I will go round tonight anyway. I could say I never saw her reply.

Saturday 24th July

I went round to her house and although some lights were on, she was clearly not in. Where on earth could she be? I waited in the car just in case she had popped to the shops or something but she didn't return and after exactly one hour I gave up. Just where could she go on a Friday evening? I will not let on that I visited but I must find out where she went and I must warn her, somehow, that her lighting makes it perfectly obvious to potential burglars that she is out for the duration. Easy pickings and we don't want anymore intruders. *Or maybe?*

Our text exchange today was insipid to say the least. Non-committal and increasingly slow responses gave me the distinct impression she was less than keen to meet today. I said I would go round. She resisted, quite skilfully. *Is she even there? Had she stayed over somewhere?* Eventually she agreed to meet, in the early evening, for a walk. We chatted but we never really got into anything. It was like two defensive chess players taking way too long to commit to anything or two boxers never throwing an actual punch, just dancing around the real issue. She said she was busy on the Sunday too, so we would talk again next week. There was something different about her that I couldn't quite put my finger on.

Sunday 25th July

I carefully went round to her house again today and found it in exactly the same state as on Friday night. I should have taken more care to examine and record its exact state to know for certain if she hadn't been home, if she is staying somewhere else. Then I remembered! How incredibly lax of me! I could simply check the tracker on her phone! As quickly as I was excited, I was then disappointed. 'Offline'. Was she onto me? Had she disabled it or was she simply, innocently offline. I obviously had no way of knowing or checking unless I could get my hands on her phone again, which at present, might be more difficult than ever. I had a look around the street, I couldn't really see anyone, and I weighed up the probabilities and the pros and cons and I broke into her house through the kitchen window. No window lock, no alarm to disable and just a sitting duck waiting to be startled. *I am sorry my darling, but I had no choice.* I was quick and efficient in disturbing things. In making it look like a simple break in. I took cash and anything that looked valuable. There wasn't much, just some bits of jewellery that didn't look up to much anyway, but that wasn't the point. I'd give her the cash back through gifts and dump her stuff in the river. I hope I haven't gone too far but *she simply has to move back towards me, and this is the only way.*

I returned home parked up, had a good look through her things and went for a walk. I took the stuff with me and waited on a bench until twilight to simply drop it in the river. Easy as pie. Nothing looked of any great value at all, most of it just looked old and she can of course over claim on her insurance like everyone does. I hope she has insurance. The cash only amounted to eighty-five quid, so hardly much of an issue given her recent pay off.

Why hasn't she texted me for help? Has she even been home yet? Is her house unsecure for the evening and maybe all night? This didn't feel like it had gone as planned at all.

Monday 26th July

No sleep last night and still nothing, so I sent an innocent text this morning just asking how she was. No reply. We are not supposed to look at personal phones in the office, so it annoys me when she doesn't reply before I arrive. She knows this.

It was past lunch when she finally text me. She said she had some bad news and could I call her when convenient. That sounded a bit cold. *I wonder what it could be?* I half mumbled that I needed to get some air and literally nobody cared, so I went for a short walk and called her. She sounded like someone trying not to be upset, trying to be strong. *But I know you best princess.* She said there had been a break in at her house. *Another one? You're not safe there my darling!* I immediately said 'When?' to try and pinpoint her movements, but maybe that wasn't the smartest question. She said she didn't know, which was interesting all the same. She had called the police and then she called her son. *Her son! He who means nothing to her!* Why weren't you in? I asked, but it felt a touch blunt so she easily ignored it and said she is to stay with her son for a while and she is to sort her house out and improve its security. That's where she has been, with her suddenly precious son. She said that not much had been taken but I took the chance to make her feel as unsafe as possible. I said she could stay with me, but it hardly seemed to reach her ear. She said she only had one truly important possession in the world and that was a necklace her grandmother had given to her. *Oops, I remember that!* She said it had been taken along with some other stuff and her voice broke as she struggled to say it. *We really love dead people's stuff, don't we?* All of this felt like it had not gone at all as I had planned and now she is further away from me than before.

Tuesday 27th July

I text her from the train again, I tried not to, but it is irresistible. This is my last week of work now and I have barely had a chance to take stock. I simply asked how she was after her nasty shock. I let her know that I was here for her in any way I could be. I also asked, gently, for her sons address so I could maybe come round and say hello. She said 'Thank you, I'm ok, just a bit shaken x' so no progress there. Stonewalled.

At work, it occurred to me that I was undertaking certain tasks now for the very last time. Things I had been doing for years. Many of which don't seem to be taken up by anyone even half willingly. I think the place and its standards will drop and then one day, perhaps weeks or even months from now, something will happen, something bad, and nobody will understand why, and it will be because standards and checks will have dropped. Someone will say 'Who's job is that?' and then they'll realise it was O'Brien who used to take care of that. He would have prevented this, they'll say.

Wednesday 28th July

I am getting a little more desperate as the distance between us is growing. I can't ask again for her sons address as that would be too needy and would alert her to my growing desperation. But there was one distinct chink of light in that I asked her about her new job, and she said she was having second thoughts. *Yes, jump on that.* I said I could talk that through with her as I only want what is best for her and in her interests. *And how.* However, she has an uncanny knack of just texting her next thought and not replying to my question. I asked how things were going with her son, just to try and open that up and to try to gain some more information about where they are but again, to no avail. *They cannot be too far.* Hopefully she will talk to me properly soon. *Is that even too much to ask now darling?*

Thursday 29th July

I pushed harder again and so she agreed to talk to me this evening after work. One last chance regarding the job I thought. One more chance to find out about the son. For all she or I know he could be trouble, he could be a danger to her. *I could work on that, plant a seed.* Work really dragged and it feels like I have already left. No one bothers me and I don't bother them, and I haven't been invited to this week's meetings which is great but also, somehow, I felt a little left out and part of me didn't like that.

When we spoke she seemed cold yet more assured. More confident, almost rehearsed and ready. I felt like she was ticking off a list of subjects and it seemed overly professional and distant. I do prefer face to face. She said she is getting on well with her son. *But how well do you know him?* She said she had decided to give the job a go and that there was a two-way probationary period. *How have we got to this?* She said she was enjoying the time out and the 'head space' and that she still needed more time to 'find herself' *Oh, what dross have you been reading darling, I am all you need.*

It all felt like a non-productive score draw at the end but there was little more I could have done. One benefit of her taking the job is that I know where it is, so I might be able to track her to her sons house from there and keep better tabs on her.

Friday 30th July

My last day officially at work. Perhaps my last day as a worker? Of course, I might work again. Maybe I can become a consultant and just point at things for money. *Give me your watch and I'll tell you the time.* Actually, I could never do that. There has to be some sense of purpose, of contribution or value.

Whilst I wasn't expecting a parade or a fanfare or anything, my ego is just big enough that I hoped for a small fuss. I mean, I have been there some years, almost all my working life, and I have put in a huge amount of effort and delivered much. Somebody brought in cakes, but that made me feel like they were celebrating my departure rather than marking the moment. *Maybe they were.* I was given four gifts. A clock, a posh pen, an unfunny 'retirement manual' and a sign I could never hang in my house that said, 'goodbye tension, hello pension'. What a waste of money. The pen is nice though. I expect everyone felt obliged to contribute and put in the minimum they could get away with. Good old peer pressure, another element of work I will not miss. I also got a card they all signed but when I looked more closely at it on the train home everyone had just put 'Good luck' or 'Best wishes' and signed their name. Nothing heartfelt or meaningful. One of my colleagues made a passing remark about just leaving when all the others had received a big pay-off and for some reason that hit me hard, almost as if I hadn't really thought about that. I felt bitter, perhaps stupid. I've missed out on thousands. I passed my interview, kept my job, missed the pay-out and then resigned. I felt a touch dizzy and confused. Surely I had thought of this before but it felt new. But now I was trapped by my own actions and there was no way back. I was literally sitting there with newly opened leaving gifts on my desk. There really didn't seem to be much emotion from anyone at all. The CEO said goodbye at about 3.30pm just before he left but he didn't suggest I could leave early or anything. He looked kind of embarrassed as if he didn't really know what to say or didn't really have anything to say.

That's that then. The irony of learning the biggest lesson regarding work on the very day it is least relevant to me is not lost on me. I wish I'd gained that knowledge on my first day, not my last.

When I got home the evening felt like some gentle anti-climax. I was unsettled. It's a strange feeling when we get what we want. *When we think we are getting what we want.* We do fixate on endings but perhaps we don't know what to do when we get there. What's next? Endings are instant but never actually endings, except one. Why wasn't I feeling excited and happy? What was my plan? *What is my plan?* I didn't even have a plan for my first evening of freedom. I didn't feel free, if anything, slightly less so.

Saturday 31st July

My first truly weightless weekend and the first of hopefully very many. Nothing at all to worry about and everything to look forward to. Yet already the weekend didn't feel like the weekend. A text or two just to see if she would reply. Some gardening, some television, some music but all in all a sense of nothingness prevailed. There didn't seem to be any urgency or much purpose to anything. The weather continues to be quite lovely though. I feel asleep in the chair with the french doors wide open. When I awoke, I didn't know where I was, what day it was or even who I was for what seemed like a few minutes. I enjoyed that spell.

Sunday 1st August

The first of the month didn't ought to be a Sunday although I'll admit that in some cultures and religions it is indeed considered to be the first day of the week. Anyway, I am no longer on any hamster wheel or calendar based rota so why do I care. I feel like gravity has left me somehow. The urgency of the clock has disappeared. The feeling of freedom I anticipated somehow feels more like I'm lost. I didn't expect this, but I will give it more time.

Monday 2nd August

She has started her new job today with all new people, including, no doubt, loads of men. I am sat here doing puzzles and going out of my mind. I text her good luck but got no reply, which I felt was more than a little rude. I decided to drive and go and see where she was but when I arrived, I parked up outside and looked to see what I could see through the windows. I didn't leave my car. I felt strangely unpleasant and more than a little bit weird, so I just turned round and came home. I even took binoculars. I won't mention it to anyone and least not her. When I got home I looked for jobs, but it made me feel tired and irritable, everything is just a word soup, and the internet is not what it pretends to be. I quite fancy working in a warehouse of something. Non-thinking physical work that tires the body and not the mind. A shift and a pay packet, that appeals. But then I wonder if I even want a job. This was not the plan at all. I need her out of there and back with me as soon as possible. Maybe she will hate it and leave quickly. Maybe there is more that I can do. Maybe I'll think properly about a job when summer is over.

Tuesday 3rd August

We had a chat over the phone in the evening. I feel like I am forcing her to talk to me now. She says she is 'loving her new job' and she 'loves the culture'. It is day two I thought, so it's very much the honeymoon period. I asked her to be cautious. *Always sow the seeds of doubt.* I am still not happy with the idea of these new, unknown to me, vultures looking at her, getting to know her and realising she is heaven sent. I feel inferior, I have no status now. My sister called today but I could barely listen. She is due in hospital later this month. There have been complications and unclear results but what does that have to do with me? She only rings me because Ms Hinchcliffe is no longer around. She asked if I would visit and so I said yes as there is only one answer to that question. But I don't want to. I didn't bother to tell my darling about it as it seemed maudlin and somehow a reflection on me. She seems unbearably lifted and energised and I don't like it. She seems to be getting even more of her confidence back and quickly. *What to do?*

Wednesday 4th August

I hate it when the schools are on holiday. The children around here need structure and the daily grind. They wander the streets with nothing to do but have boundless energy to burn. They become threatening all too easily. Is there nothing for them to do other than to try to procure alcohol or to push over an elderly lady's bin. I feel, at times, like they are trapping me in my house, and I feel like building walls or erecting fences to protect my territory.

Thursday 5th August

I went out shopping today. Something I never get any pleasure out of, and I cannot really understand how acquiring stuff in a stifled, air-conditioned environment, pleases other so much. I was seemingly surrounded by couples, with their arms linked or with their hands in each other's back pockets. Why do they have to display their affections so publicly? Are they engaging in some sort of showing off? They wave their shopping bags around at each other as if trying to achieve some sort of one upmanship on each other. I imagine they all go back to their leased vehicles and smile at their own private number plates. It is one of a series of grotesque rituals that is now commonplace. They are chasing something they can never attain, they chase approval from people they do not know, or hardly know. I think it was Freud who said, 'The more you know, the less you need to show'. I keep myself to myself.

I was incredibly lucky to find a necklace almost exactly the same as the one her grandmother gave her. I realised the gesture might appear slightly desperate, but surely she would see the romance, the love in it. It cost quite a tidy sum and I didn't even ask about returning it as I never considered I might have to. I always feel like I pay too much for things and I think that is because of the general smugness of the sales people.

I text her to say I needed to see her, however only briefly, because I had something important to give to her. She said she would be at home at 7pm if I wanted to call round. It read like she wasn't at home permanently but maybe I'm just reading too much into it.

I arrived, had dressed smartly and I had put on my best aftershave, the one I knew she liked. She opened the door with a palpable degree of trepidation. That hurt a little. I said 'hello' and she said 'hello' but the door wasn't even fully open. I sensed maybe someone was inside, but who? I explained that I understood her feeling of loss over her grandmother's necklace. *I didn't.* And as I explained I had gone to some trouble to replace it I opened the dainty little box and showed her what I had bought. The evening light seemed to give it extra credence. Her reaction was unexpected to say the least. She seemed to go completely white, faint even. I was genuinely concerned. Maybe she was overcome by my kindness. She was physically shaken as she looked at it. I felt that my gesture could get us back on track, that it was a stroke of genius. It still might. I didn't feel the need to offer more words or even to push any agenda of us being a proper couple again as I thought time, following the gesture, would work for me and not against me. She was literally aghast. She held it, she looked at it, she looked at me and she tried to speak but nothing came out. The look she gave me was one of shock, I think. Then she seemed to snap back into life, she grabbed the box and the necklace, let out some sort of shriek and slammed the door in my face. I gently called her name. I just stood there. I tried to call her three times and then I spoke through the letterbox. I let her know how I understood that this might be all too much and maybe the surprise was a little overwhelming and that maybe we should have talked about it first. My gesture appeared to have really hit home. Then I left. I text her on the way home to let her know she could take as much time as possible and that I was happy and ready to talk in any time frame she felt right.

I went to bed happy, I felt like I had really touched her, really moved her and I hoped this was the turning point of her coming back to me. *I'll be as patient as a tree when it comes to regaining your love, my darling.*

Friday 6th August

Nothing from her today, which surprised me a little. The temptation to text her is almost constant, given I have very little to actually do. I took a look at my finances and re-arranged my spreadsheets. I went out to buy some food but I was restless, ever waiting for that golden message from her to say she loved me. I yearned and craved the all forgiving hug, the kiss of amnesty.

Nothing came. *Nothing.*

Saturday 7th August

I was pleased that this Saturday still felt like a Saturday, like a different day from the week. We really do have traditions engrained into us, don't we?

By 11am I could hold my water no longer. I text her to say 'Let's talk x' and I anxiously awaited her reply. I tried to pretend I had stuff to do by making a list but even writing things down didn't fool me. I approached the list and each task upon it with a false sense of urgency. I cannot fool myself.

My phone finally pinged at 1.12pm. 'I'm really busy today, but could we meet in the park, tomorrow, at maybe 1pm ish?' No kiss. Plus, it felt like a swerve of lunch or dinner so I pushed no further and just agreed. *It is at least, something.*

Sunday 8th August

When we met, I noticed what I assumed to be her son, had given her a lift and was waiting in the car. He tried to look like he was not watching us. I enquired about him and offered to go over and say hello but her refusal was brisk and certain and laced with some sort of shame. She barely looked me in the eye at all. She seemed to keep looking back at the car park. I asked about the necklace, and why it had upset her so much. I said I assumed she was just overwhelmed but she said she didn't want to talk about it. I felt I had overestimated my progress of last Thursday and our full union now seemed further away than I had hoped. She did perk up a little when I asked about her new job. It took all of my acting ability to look genuinely pleased and excited for her, as that was the only reasonable response. She mentioned a 'Tom'. I asked about 'us' but she soon moved the subject on. I asked her round for dinner, for lunch and felt like I was sounding increasingly desperate. Eventually I gave up and she went back to her son's car.

I was confused, and on the way home I was angry. *I am getting more than a little fed up of playing the long game.*

Monday 9th August

It's Monday but it doesn't feel like Monday and that was supposed to be a good thing. I just felt a bit lost again today. *Already.* It's nice to sleep in a little but it's not so nice to have no purpose in your day, nothing to really get up for. The removal of the irritation of work and its stresses is good but it feels like the removal of a negative rather than the addition of a positive. That thought made me see that I needed to find something, something to do, and it could be anything I wanted. We are not used to having a such a free hand of choice and it feels overwhelming to have to consider so many possibilities. So instead, I just watched an old black and white film, ate some toast and fell asleep. I am old before my time.

Tuesday 10th August

I had to fill a form in today, one of those online forms that only allows certain answers. *Well, you certainly must fit into one of our categories.* Except I didn't and when it came to employment status, the only option I could choose was unemployed. This was then swiftly followed up by having to declare my annual earnings as zero. I can't say that left me with a good feeling and the sentiment hung around in my mind for most of the day. *Is that what I am now?*

Wednesday 11th August

I was in a world of my own today when I heard the doorbell go. It shook me to my senses and brought me back into the real world. As I opened the door, standing there, in absolute innocence, was a small boy, most likely on his school holidays. My natural suspicion put me on my guard and I expected a trick or some sort of prank but his smile radiated a naivety that was pure. He seemed to wait for me to say hello, which I duly did and then he, with some nervousness yet pride, delivered a mini speech. Shoulders back and the Queens english. This young entrepreneur was looking for small jobs to do in return for some pay. My instincts would always be to send such an urchin away but this young chap had something quite captivating. I am no judge of a child's age, given my lack of any experience with them, but I imagined him to be about ten years old. I asked him if he would like to clean my car. This felt safe to me as he would be outside and we wouldn't have to interact and he seemed delighted at the suggestion. He stood there with his childish excitement at his sale but seemingly had no next step in mind. He had no bucket and no idea.

As I continued sorting through things and cleaning and reorganising, my eye kept catching him working studiously on my car. His sense of urgency, his sense of pride seemed to radiate through the window. It matched his total lack of experience. He was just a ball of enthusiasm. I couldn't help but smile outwardly when I realised he had started with such zeal yet he had failed to negotiate his fee. His approach to life, his boundless happiness and keenness gave me some sort of fillip and another part of me wanted to talk to him. Maybe we would be good for each other. I could teach him about the world and he could infect me with his seemingly unlimited positivity. But then, that sort of thing might be frowned upon or misunderstood by passers by, so I let the feeling pass. That brought something new to the fore. A sadness, a realisation that not only will I never have children of my own now but in fact I do not have any children at all in my life. I did wonder, for while, what sort of father I would be? I thought again about my father and what sort of role model he was to me. When you are young, your parents are your friends, the police, judge and jury. They are everything and I recall having absolute faith in them, their opinions and their actions. You trust them in a way you will never trust again.

He finished cleaning the car. It was hardly a good job and in actual fact, his efforts made me visit the car wash soon after, but he had tried and he had tried hard. He has shown his face, gone out into the world and he had put effort into his day and tried to make something of himself and so I lied when I told him he had done a fantastic job. He beamed with a youthful pride that was more than worthy of such a white lie. See, it is sometimes right to lie. Then he just stood there, awaiting his fee I expect. I had no idea how much to pay him so I asked 'How much is that then?' he just shrugged and as he did, he smiled a smile to melt all tired hearts. 'How does five pounds sound?' I enquired. His reaction suggested I might have exceeded his expectations. His feet could barely stay in place. I delivered the fiver and his hand touched mine. Such soft skin, such small fingers. Hands of little experience of life. And then he literally skipped away down my drive, his voice somewhat paralysed by his bounty. I closed the door and reckoned I might see him again. Surely, I would be a repeat customer. But then I had a thought that drew a tear to each eye. I would perhaps never see him again and maybe I would never see such innocence, such untouched beauty ever again. I forgot to ask him his name too.

Thursday 12th August

Sometimes you just need a day when you do nothing much at all, when there is little or no adrenaline and no specific nor rigid agenda. A day when the brain and the body can recuperate. I seem to be having a lot of these sort of days at the moment.

I wondered where I could drive to, to get the car dirty again and then I could park it at the end of the drive for him to see he was needed again. Though I began to doubt his innocence to a degree. We teach them lies early, we tell them lies. We corrupt them. *Santa is a lie.*

Friday 13th August

I might grow a beard. I've never had a beard. That's hardly *something to do* though, is it.

Saturday 14th August

It is Saturday but the reward of its arrival has all but dissipated. It is another day just like all the others. Not a peep from my love, nothing. I text her three times to ask if she might like to meet up and do anything. She said she would let me know about maybe something tomorrow. Could she be any less committed?

Sunday 15th August

I reviewed all of my charity direct debits today, as I need to trim down my outgoings now that I don't have any actual incomings. It was terribly difficult to choose between elephants, rhinos and pandas, so I cancelled them all but left the more generic RSPCA one in place. I did notice that most of them are to protect the animal kingdom and their habitats and not so much have I committed to helping actual fellow human beings. I have always been of sound judgement. I felt like I had consolidated my charity effort quite well and then for some reason, at the end, I started a new one with the NSPCC. 'Children need protecting from the adults' should be their slogan, or maybe, 'Children need protecting from the future'? They don't need protecting from themselves, so they.

Monday 16th August

Having blanked me all weekend she suggested we have a 'chat' on the phone this evening. *I have to fit in with her busy work schedule now, don't I.* She constantly refers to her new boss 'Tom' in ways I'd prefer she didn't. There is a familiarity there that I could start to despise. My tactic at this moment is to keep her talking about him so I can get more and more useful information and detail. Keep her comfortable until I know what I need to know. At the same time, I can work on her to be suspicious of him, to warn her of what men at work can be like. *Vultures who see their prey.* This is a situation that shouldn't even exist and now I might need to handle it. What can I find out about this 'Tom' character?

Other than that, the conversation felt transactional yet maybe a tad warmer than recently, so I'll regard it as progress, a step in the right direction. *It is better than nothing.*

Tuesday 17th August

Tom appears on their company website. He is the COO of the company. His profile picture is so manufactured and false it would be more at home on a cheesy 90's American sit-com. Big collar, pink shirt, manicured hair and lots of perfect white teeth. His smile is so false it looks like it could fall off. Thanks to his standing and status, his home address is available via companies house. I have you Tom, I have the advantage now. *I have cards.*

Wednesday 18th August

I went for a walk and considered whether I miss work or not. I concluded that I definitely don't want to go back to work, as the work I could visualise was the office I have only just left. I don't miss the commute yet I wondered, somewhat bizarrely, how my fellow commuters might be faring. I could never go back now that I have left anyway, bridges, if not entirely burnt, have been somewhat damaged by my trampling over them to get away. Maybe I could do the commute and back one day, but then, what would I do with all the time in between? It will have all moved on without me by now anyway. I also don't want to have to start again somewhere new. I feel too old to be new at anything and if I'm honest I am a little bit scared of starting afresh. But I also feel like I don't want to not work. I might try for some temporary or agency work to stay occupied, to bring in a few pounds, to allow me to have something to put on forms or to say when people ask, and also something not too permanent, just to last until my princess is fully back with me and back on board with our plan to move to the Southwest coast. Something to fit that bill, to at least refuel my ego, my standing, a little. I have no idea how to find such work though, but I'll try again and look online without quickly getting that sickly feeling from each and every search result. My money feels like it only ever reduces now, and I wasn't really prepared for that even though it was blindingly obvious this would happen. I don't really know what I want or how to get it. *This is her fault.*

Thursday 19th August

I hoovered again today and I had ticked off my to do list before ten. I looked out of the window to see if my car cleaner might come back and I filled the bird feeder to see if my robin might return. I didn't even see a spider or it's web today. I had a nap in the early afternoon and listened to a Radio 4 play afterwards.

Friday 20th August

It's Friday and so the working community will be all anticipatory about the coming weekend and this will manifest itself into the best working day of the week. They are slaves to the system so how come, sometimes, I feel like I envy them or that I miss that part of working life. Have I become so indoctrinated into this social norm that I can never escape, I can never just be? Is this like a long serving prisoner who actually doesn't want to be released as he knows no other way of life? Does anyone ever intend this to happen to its general population, or is it just an unhappy consequence of a system nobody ever intended to build. Capitalism, that's what this is, and I am branded and scarred just like the prisoner I now realise I am.

Saturday 21st August

My phoned pinged early this morning and my excitement quickly changed to bitterness and abject disappointment as it turned out to be my sister and not my love. She seems to be trying to give me a step-by-step account of each stage of her treatment and the view of her possible recovery. *Boring.* I replied to each text as I had nothing else to do and I somehow reckoned that using my phone and texting might bring about a text from my love. It didn't and another weekend is passing without my seeing her. I decided not to text her to try and make her second guess me for a change and to try and make her text me. *Nothing.*

Sunday 22nd August

I decided to try and plan next week more carefully. I decided to try and create some goals and then within those, some milestones. It somehow felt false though. I do not know why. After a snooze, I wondered whether it is a sense of my life being on hold, my waiting for my darling to come to her senses and come back to me so that we can put the real plan in place. Yes, that was it, my plans are temporary and false as much deeper down, I have a real, more meaningful plan that is just waiting to spring into action and bring my happiness back. It will bring my completeness back. *It will bring my life back.*

Monday 23rd August

I drove to perfect Tom's house to take a look today. Not so perfect as it turns out. His garden is a mess. I'd say he is a spender, flash but not a careful or hard-working man. She will tire of him in time. I considered a minor act of vandalism or maybe a warning through his letterbox but decided they were poor moves in the bigger game and it is best to keep myself out of sight completely to ensure I have the upper hand for when I might need to make a more meaningful, more important move. *Go carefully Tom.*

Tuesday 24th August

My sister text to remind me it is her operation today and that this is a key moment. *Yes, I know because you keep texting me.* I tried to think of more than 'Good luck' to put in my text back but I just couldn't be bothered, so I just went with that. No reply. Deep down, I do actually hope she is okay, I do hope she receives some luck but it feels very little to do with me. I think when a text looks like it's from a standard template it loses something of its meaning. I did have a brief text exchange with my darling and she seemed to know some details I hadn't told her. Is she directly in touch with my sister?

Wednesday 25th August

The text exchange continued today. *Progress.* And so I asked her how work was going today. Finally, she had agreed to come round for tea following my invitation. She would see how the house is spick and span and how well I am doing. It would give her a glimpse of how her life, our life together, could be. She wasn't wearing the new necklace but then she never wore the old one so I didn't think anything much of it. Maybe she simply replaced it for the old one in her drawer, like before. The conversation seemed to skim our issues, the things I really wanted to talk about and she, somewhat formally just ate, drink and spoke. She seemed a little on guard and not relaxed. I asked about her son and I stupidly asked about the father again and then immediately felt like I was pushing all the wrong buttons. I half joked that I could get a job at the same place as her. It was a small test. Her face screwed up with some sort of instinctive disgust. I have my answer. She didn't mention Tom. *Conspicuous by his absence, I'd say.*

Thursday 26th August

I felt obliged and indeed forced to visit my sister today on what can only be described as her death bed. I wonder what is in her will. Will that be relevant, is she really dying? I went alone as this is one aspect of life I do not wish to increasingly share with my darling. It's just morbid. I did wonder if she would have wanted to come with me, they did seem to somewhat hit it off at Ms Hinchcliffe's funeral. My sister had the absolute audacity to forgive me. What an act of asserting control, I thought. I was so enraged I wanted to end it there and then by strangulation or smothering. *How dare she even consider that I needed forgiving.* I didn't make her ill in the first place. I didn't tell her not to save some money in case she might need it. I didn't perform the operation unsuccessfully. If she is to die, she is to die on her own terms and as nature has intended. A cruel hand dealt maybe, but many others have faced worse. I'm disappointed it took me so long to respond to her, I am normally quicker. I stood there with the only living blood relative I have left in my life and I said 'I cannot be forgiven for something that is nothing to do with me. If your time is nigh, I hope you find peace on the other side'. I tried my best to conceal my smile, but I did feel it on my lips a little. She had just enough energy in her to pull a face of astonishment. She needed me to be the villain, she needed to be able to blame me, to be the reason this all happened, in part or maybe in whole. I am damned if I would give her that. I am an innocent bystander and tomorrow, or at least very soon after she will most likely be dead and gone. I said my goodbyes and she said 'bastard' as I left. Not very becoming for a lady I thought and no way to leave things. *May her bitterness erode her final moments.* It was also fortuitous that there was no need to assist the process. The risk of any intervention was far too high and for so little reward. I will let time and fate take care of this and looking at her face, it won't take them long. Just a short number of days at most. Hopefully she is too weak to change her will and I will now get an even greater share of things then even I felt I was owed. *Funny how things turn out.* Who was it that said, 'Life is but a shipwreck of our plans?' Absolute nonsense. Ha.

Friday 27th August

The hospital phoned to say my sister had died in the early hours. *The grim reaper can be so efficient.* Even beyond the grave they have you running after them. Hopefully her will shall surface soon. I can wait, no rush. Anyway, it's another anniversary to mark on the calendar and one which I can, hopefully, quickly forget. No card to buy, no action to take. Maybe I'll ironically buy a little something with her money each year. I was surprised to find that after finally hearing the news I was a little bit sad though. I said I'd be over later. I tried to sound all sorrowful and reflective. I can act, but no real motivation here. Anyway, I was mid-way through a good film and so I watched the end before setting off. Films don't have good endings anymore, they tend to have good beginnings now.

I had to tell my darling all about this. It seemed natural to use it to lever some compassion, some sense of togetherness, maybe some sympathy. She would see that I needed her. We have been on such a rocky road recently and we've had such a bad run of news. *Can I make this a turning point?* I said we needed to speak but that I could only do it face to face. Draw her in. She came round quite quickly so it delayed me going to the hospital. *The dead can wait, can't they?* She said she was devastated for me. *Devastated?* I took the pity, the consolation for all it was worth. She didn't seem inclined to hug or kiss me though. She said she would like to pay her respects at the funeral and I saw that as another chance for us to be together and for most of the day so I agreed with some sort of sad reflective, contemplative gesture but really, I was just pleased she wanted to be with me for the day.

Saturday 28th August

My darling came round again and we chatted about my sister. I had played the sympathy card to get her round but she hardly came through the door. It took her 25 minutes to even take her coat off. It all feels so cold now. She is obsessed with work and I sense that I am becoming ever more peripheral and unimportant in her life. She seems to have renewed energy and ever increasing confidence so I asked her if the police had been in touch recently and that knocked her down a peg or two. She seemed a little shocked I had asked and so I took advantage and pushed the point home. 'They'll be back for you soon, no doubt' I said. 'They haven't seemed to follow up or talk to anyone else' I said. I saw the brokenness reappear in her eyes and face. It felt awful, yet necessary to bring her worst stresses to the surface. But it is those same stresses that will make her need a partner in life, a protector. At the same time, I do miss who she used to be and I want her back as all mine again. How did we get here? I preferred her without all this confidence. She needed me more then. I'm not letting her go though. *She is still mine.* And so, she goes nowhere on anyone's terms but mine.

Before she left, we talked about my sister again and at one point she picked my hand up with hers and I felt something. I looked at her and smiled a little smile. I tried to appear, gentle, caring and vulnerable. Vulnerability creates bonds. It seemed to work but only a little.

After she left, I felt a bit better but then I started to think about her talking to her male colleagues at work and her new boss 'Tom'. All young and in fancy shirts with their swaggering wit and I hate it. I felt the anger rising.

Sunday 29th August

I decided to go and investigate this Tom character again today. I need to understand him a little more and assess the threat. I thought I might see him at his house. Maybe I would see if he is married or co-habiting. Hopefully I'd find out he is gay. I sat away from the house and just watched. Nothing happened, no sign of anyone at all, and then, as if by some lucky twist of fate, he got into his car. One of those German sports cars that look expensive. He keeps it in the garage so he's not all bad. I'm not sure why, but I followed him. He entered the local supermarket and so, a few paces behind, I followed him in. He took a trolley and seemed to have a list. Again, he's not all bad then. I thought I could find out a lot by what he buys and I could still be completely unknown to him. I enjoyed watching him, knowing he was completely oblivious to my presence. I saw him collect all the staple items of a family weekly shop. He was definitely shopping for more than one person. And then I saw the defining item of the shop, a big box of nappies. I couldn't help but grin. He has at least one baby. Therefore, he must have a wife. He is a man with a young family. But just as the splendour of all this news was sinking through my excited skin, I remembered what life, what men, are like. He will be sex starved, he will be sleep starved. The romance in his relationship will have been replaced with a grind, a task-based existence he won't want to adjust to. His ego, his cravings for affection, for fun and for intimacy will be at their highest. His status will allow him to belief he deserves, no, is entitled to, whatever he wants and he will be pursuing my princess with an increased verve. He will be using work as a way of getting away from it for a few days. He will create conferences or book ones he doesn't need to go to and he'll be insisting, as the boss, that my darling attends. He'll trap her. Then he'll create intimate dinners where he will work all of his smarmy charm and deliver all of his oily anecdotes to get closer to her. She will be his prey and she will not be able to exercise her own free will.

I drove my trolley into his, as if accidently, just to fire a warning shot. I said, 'oh sorry' and then I simply abandoned my half-filled trolley and went home. *Something must be done.*

Monday 30th August

It is Bank Holiday today although I'm not sure just what it has to do with Banks anymore. Most of the branches have shut around here and, of course, everyone does their banking online nowadays so this is yet another tradition that refuses to die and has absolutely no relevance in our new world. An 'online holiday' is more in order, and would be more welcome, but then what would the zombies do all day? Turn off the Wi-Fi I say, just for twenty four hours. Could you imagine?

Tuesday 31st August

I received confirmation of the arrangements for my sister's funeral today. I can barely be bothered to go but my focus will be on the opportunity it affords me with my darling. I called her, yes just called her with no introductory text and she just picked up and said hello like it was the nineteen nineties all over again. *How refreshing.* I confirmed the dates and times with her and she did sound compassionate and that made me feel better. The decency in her is my advantage. I'll need my full acting repertoire with me, I'll need to be a mourning brother, abandoned son, lonely boyfriend but with lashings of resolve and no self-pity. She is to see a gentle warrior, a brave, strong man who, despite being dealt a number of killer blows, still functions, nay contributes to society. A whole day to be with her, an opportunity that I must make the most of.

Wednesday 1st September

She has reflected and unfortunately, she had decided to make her own way to the service and back. This is a most unwelcome and disappointing development as the time in the car was crucial to my plan. It would have certainly been the best time to work on her one on one with no fear at all of interruption. I would have been able to plan my performance. A time where I could work through the gears and make some real headway. I insisted I pick her up and take her home, to save her from effort, but she said that her arrangements were in place and couldn't be changed. All by text. I hate texting, it's a necessary evil but it is so cold and transactional and it gave me no inroads to exploit, you get no hint of someone wavering via text.

Thursday 2nd September

It was the day my sister was finally burnt to a crisp. I honestly couldn't wait for the casket to start its journey into the furnace, just to make absolutely sure she was all gone. Just how many funerals can I go to? I feel like I know the service to the point where I could perform it myself. A new career beckons, perhaps. In the excitement, I'd start to rush, I'd be terrible. The next one I have to go to might be my own. At least I don't need to ask for compassionate leave anymore. It was getting a bit embarrassing. There's nobody else left now that is anywhere near ready. And then my ever ready brain considered the worst case scenario and I just couldn't bear to think that one day I would have to go to my darling's funeral.

If I go first, she will be all alone and open to prey. If she goes first, I will be all alone and lost. Maybe it's best if we both go together, on the same day, at the same time? *Now there's a thought.*

It was surprisingly well attended. I received lots of knowing yet faux caring looks from closed mouthed strangers. Bless him they thought. My thoughts are with you, they thought. *I'll never see you again, I thought. What's in the will, I thought.*

My darling was annoyingly pre-occupied with the occasion. She made more effort to speak to complete strangers than she did to me. She said her son was to pick her up at five. Directly from the wake, which was annoying. This son of hers is proving to be a difficulty, an obstruction and god knows who he is, or what he thinks, or indeed what he is filling her head with. I did make the most of every second with her I could. I even found a false tear and coupled this with some shaking. *I gave it my all.* I said how the passing of my sister had made me see sense, I explained how it had made me see the error of my ways recently, how indeed it had made me think about what truly matters and that none of us know what time we have left and so we cannot waste another moment. I all but begged her forgiveness and for her and I to get back on track. I did feel like she was wavering. She touched my knee with her leather gloved hand at one point. She said she needed to think. *That's what she always says. She never used to need to think this much, when we first got together.*

Friday 3rd September

Today's gift from heaven, or wherever, was for my darling to come round to see me and then pop to the shops. Guilt driven behaviour but who cares. I'm chipping away and have clearly made some progress. I think she was concerned about me after yesterday. *Ah bless.* I could hardly believe my luck when she left her phone on the kitchen worktop. As cool as I liked, the moment she left, I could hardly wait to see what is going on in her life. I could establish more than a few answers to nagging questions just by looking at her texts, messages, emails and photos. But my worst suspicions might well have been realised as she has changed her access code so I couldn't get in. There is another way, *there must be.* But why, oh why has she felt the need to change the code?

When she came back, she seemed incredibly alarmed that she had left without it. I had placed it back right where she left it and I pretended I had no idea at all it was even there. I even helped her look for it. *Oh, there it is look.* She looked at it for quite a long time and then somewhat buried it back into her handbag. *The shopping was so kind, I said. Please stay a while, I said. She is on her way back to me.*

Saturday 4th September

A rainy Saturday brought with it a void of nothingness. After all the activity of the week, I seemed to be in some state of abeyance between what has just gone and what is next to come. I sent her a text, simply to say, 'Thank you for coming round yesterday, so kind and so lovely to see you x'. There was no reply so after an hour or so I sent another one that said, 'I hope we can see each other again soon, I'll always love you x' and after I had sent the second one I wish I hadn't as it was badly worded. I received no reply to either so then I started to wonder who indeed she is texting today and what they are saying and it brought down my mood terribly. Especially when I thought more about her changing her access code.

Sunday 5th September

I decided to make a big Sunday dinner today, with all of the trimmings. I was doing it anyway, just because I wanted to. When things were prepared and the cooking had started I sent her a text. I tried to capture a mood of, 'I'm so busy, making a dinner, please come round as there is way too much for one'. It said 'I really fancied making a proper old fashioned Sunday dinner today. There is far too much, please feel free to come round x' but after I had sent it, I realised there isn't a direct question there, no call to action so no need to reply. *So, are you coming my darling, have you read it, will you reply?*

Neither did she turn up nor did I get a reply. I will be able to get about four days dinners out of this, this week, so it wasn't a total waste of time. I am a good cook.

Monday 6th September

I get seventy five percent of the estate after costs and fees are deducted. The other twenty five goes to charity. So that's about fair I reckon. *All's well that ends well.* I am finally to get what is due plus a nice chunk of my sisters money. How ironic, I thought, given that she had asked me for a tidy sum that would have delayed this windfall and extended our pointless relationship. This might mean I don't have to bother with work again at all. I felt positively chipper at the news.

Tuesday 7th September

The most ridiculous thing happened to me today. How odd life can be. I went out for a long walk and decided to go down the edge of the woods as I like to feel alone with nature and I like to see the birds and the trees. I was about halfway down and something caught my eye. At first, it looked like half buried newspaper and as I got closer it looked like tin foil. *Intriguing.* It wasn't difficult to sweep away the thin layer of earth on top with my hands and to discover what was a ridiculous amount of money, along with some carefully wrapped square parcels just looking back at me. I felt excited and had a rush of adrenaline. Nobody was around. It might have been sensible to just walk on by, but I had disturbed it now and would have to spend more time reconcealing it than to just pop it all in my bag. I had one of those 'bags for life' in my pocket, the type that wraps itself into a little ball. I couldn't resist popping it all in my bag and then just walking on as normal. I kept looking around but there was literally nobody anywhere near me at all. It was all quite exciting and thrilling. It was hard not to run. I felt like I was on a television drama and I felt like skipping, an urge I haven't had since I was a child. It wasn't really on a normal walking route. It must have been placed there purposely. Maybe for someone to pick up, or maybe as a hiding place for someone to return to. I kept looking for any sign of someone. I literally couldn't see another soul. As easy as you like I had just stumbled upon this stash, picked it up and left no trace whatsoever of my being there. The temptation to further explore my stash immediately was overtaken by the much more sensible thought to act very normal and wait until I got home. I checked again and again that nobody was around and I was certain that I could just leave undetected, undetectable. I tried to think of a plan. Such fun, such adventure. Maybe just hide it for a while, see if there is anything on the local news and then spend the cash bit by bit. Why and in what circumstance would it be on the news? I don't mix in such circles, well, in any real circles at all and so I'd never find out if anyone was angry or looking for it. Anyway, I was the perfect assailant, who would suspect me? I have no use for the drugs, if that's what they are, and could never contemplate trying to use or sell them. I just don't have that inclination or indeed the skills.

When I arrived home, I put the bag and its contents into a spare wheelie bin I have in the back garden. When the original wheelie bins were delivered, I didn't get one so I called the council. Then, the next day and the day after they delivered two, so I have a spare. I keep compost and other gardening bit and pieces in there, so it felt like a safe place. Hopefully the smell of the other stuff would put off any potential sniffer dog and being right at the back of the garden, there's no way the aroma could ever travel that far. I might pop out later, just before dark, to look at my new treasure a little closer. I wonder just how much cash there is. I could give it to charity or maybe do some good with it. *I am Robin Hood.*

Wednesday 8th September

She's still distant. I am sure her head been turned by someone else and Tom is my chief suspect. Greasy, oily Tom with his silver tongue and his need to feel powerful. With his fancy car and his power over her as her new boss. I knew this would happen if she went back to work. Yes, Tom with his pink shirts, his white teeth, his silly hair and his big salary. It's the power of the boss, the authority. He wants to be with her so much and he'll try all his tricks. *Something must be done.*

In the afternoon, I went and looked at my find. I hardly dare. It was all quite a thrill. There was just over eight grand in cash but most of it is in fifty pound notes, which will make it stand out, so I'll need to think about that. There are two packages of something. It must be drugs, what else could it be? They are sealed and packaged very tightly but look just like the drugs parcels you see on television dramas, so they must be one drug or another. Cocaine? Heroin? I have literally no idea what to do with them, but it seems like a stupid risk to take them back. I should hang onto them for a short while just in case I was seen and in case I need to give them back to save my kneecaps, but at some point I need to dispose of them. The trusty river, full of secrets it can never tell, will be my saviour again. Somebody, somewhere must be really angry about losing all of this. The street value, if that is the right term, of these drugs must be high as the packages are not small. Plus eight grand in cash. This scared me more than a little. This is not, at all, my world. I'll just chuck them in the river when the time seems right and I'll be careful with the money. Gently, gently, but some fun and a thrill too.

We had tea together at the cafe and I asked her directly if there was anyone else and her answer of 'no' was far from convincing in my view. I stared at her, and she weakened. There is someone else. I knew it. This does not end here. And why does her son suddenly now have to escort her everywhere. Why is he always there, in his car, watching us and creating some sort of ticking clock whenever we meet?

Thursday 9th September

I've decided to take a trip. Now is the time both in a 'moment' way and in a 'big picture' way. The summer is departing and I am free of employment, so it is now. My princess needs breathing space and perhaps, although it sounds a tad arrogant, she needs to see how life is without me, out of reach, she needs to miss me a touch. My plan is for absence to make her heart grow fonder and for jealousy to give it an extra gentle push. I will tell her I am taking a few days away to Devon. I will rebook 'our cottage'. I will tell her I have a 'project' that needs quiet, contemplative concentration (*I don't*) and I will be just a little bit vague as to whether I will be alone or accompanied. I can't say I really want to go as it will be a bit of a pain, a bit difficult and maybe a little bit of a waste of money, but it will do me, us, good and might just adjust my perspective a little and hopefully hers. I have decided that I will go and see my Dad's grave at the same time. Just to see if I can connect a little with him and then I will spend a few nights down at the cottage. I will let my darling know gently and I will come back refreshed and ready for any new chapter life might wish to throw my way. *It feels right.*

I've put a load of stuff in the wheelie bin, on top of 'the stuff' just to be on the safe side.

Friday 10th September

I woke up and the feeling had not passed. In fact, I felt an unusual resolution to push on with my plan. I checked online regarding availability, and fate, for once, dealt me a kind blow. Not only is our cottage available, it seems that it is subject to a late cancellation and therefore it is available from Monday night at a knockdown price. I booked it for four nights and confirmed and paid in full there and then. *How bold, how assertive.* This made me feel purposeful, decisive and like I was a man of certainty, a man with a plan with somewhere to go. I hadn't felt like this in a while and so I went for a little walk to revel in the feeling before it, like everything else, passed. The main thing I planned for on my walk was how to tell her in the best way to get her inquisitive juices flowing. I didn't go anywhere near where the I found the stuff and I perhaps never will again. *Maybe she will be desperate to come too?*

Saturday 11th September

The text is ready to send. I actually wrote it out onto paper to get it just right. This time, a text was the right medium.

'Hello there. I am going away for a few days to get my head together. The only place that felt right was our cottage. I have something to do which requires clear headspace. I will be thinking about what truly matters to me. I do love you x'

I think that hits the right note and so was pleased to send it. For the first time in my life, I text her without feeling the need to instantly look for her reply. I wanted this to soak in. I wanted her to really think about the numerous aspects of message I had sown. The longer I didn't receive a reply, the better. But then, by late evening I started to fail to understand why there was no reply at all.

Sunday 12th September

I starting packing today and preparing. I felt I could take enough food with me as to not need to food shop in a town and shop I didn't know. I also think I had convinced myself that I did indeed have a project to undertake and it took some time for me to realise I have nothing at all to do when I arrive. I have some books to read, some walks I can enjoy but I am hardly a painter or a writer or anything like that. I am sure the time will fly by and that I will enjoy the solitude, the head space and the chance to move away from my normal routine.

I cut the grass to ensure it wouldn't look unkempt upon my return. I've always enjoyed cutting the grass and I love my square, flat lawn and the stripes I can leave on it. I have a good mower.

Still no reply. Is she thinking, has she read it, has she considered I might not be alone? I maybe, didn't get that particular point across well enough.

Monday 13th September

I set off today as to avoid any Monday morning work traffic. Quite the benefit of my new lifestyle that I don't need to get sucked into that particular displeasure. I can only check in after 3pm, so I needed to ensure I wouldn't be early. I couldn't decide whether to leave the curtains open or shut so I left half open and closed half which only seemed like an odd thing to do when I was half way down the motorway. I made sure everything was locked, the house had no food or liquids that would go out of date and I ensured that some lighting would come on in the evening. I can't contemplate a burglary or anything like that. I made sure the gate was locked and that the bins were behind it. If the police or anyone did find the stuff in the other bin, I would just plead ignorance, like someone else must have stashed it there. I think I could get away with that. I mean, I'm hardly a drugs baron in anyone's imagination.

Tuesday 14th September

It was a strange night. I felt like there were no rules, no guidance as to what to do. I felt like I was floating, that I needed a least a simple structure. What on earth do people do on holiday? Still no text back. Is this good or bad? What exactly did I want? I have no plan and no home comforts. I wondered if my house, my garden, were alright. I sat and made a sandwich and put the television on. I had driven all this way to watch programmes I could have watched at home. In fact, there was less choice than at home both in terms of what I could watch, eat or do.

I thought about James. I felt like I wanted to set fire to his bin or at least do something but I couldn't decide what I wanted out of it so I stopped my childish plotting. *If you are to do something, do something worth it. Send a real message.* That got me thinking about smarmy, greasy Tom again and his dirty intentions. I stopped my brain thinking, visualising what they would look like together. I tortured myself as I thought about him undressing her. She looked like she was enjoying it but she doesn't understand she has been trapped. The spider wants his fly. This raised a new level of anger and determination in me. *Something must be done.*

This is not what this trip is supposed to be about. I should have just pretended to come.

Wednesday 15th September

I slept soundly, which was pleasing. I found the total quiet a bit unnerving at first but it clearly didn't last. I felt an urgency to enjoy my time which felt nice. Certainly that is better than feeling listless. I set off on a walk after breakfast and thought I'd walk about four miles and then just head back. About a mile and a half out, my phone pinged. *It must be her.* Her text said 'When are you back?'. *That was a little unexpected.* Such a long time and such a dull reply. Why did she want to know that? What was she planning? *My house is empty.* Had I inadvertently given her the upper hand? Should I say a date and time much later than was true and then I could sit in waiting for her, *for them. Take your time, think.*

I replied when I got back to the cottage. *Don't always reply so quickly.* Stick to the plan of letting her know I was busy, focussed, that I have other things, and maybe someone new on my mind. It is good to reply slowly and indeed, somewhat falsely. Another of those useful lies I thought. Lying gets such a bad press. It is such a useful tool to navigate modern life and I expect it has always been so, ever since we learned to talk. Everyone lies, probably, every day so who will take it upon themselves to be the first truly honest human? Nobody, nobody in their right mind anyway. 'Back late Monday' I replied. A reply I enjoyed. No concern for her. I am focused you see. No more detail than needed. *I am occupied you see.* No neediness. *You want me back now, don't you?*

Plus, I have a few days in hand to see what she is up to, what she plans to do and I'll just be at home both ready and prepared for what she has in mind.

Thursday 16th September

I started to think about going home today and I managed to put my anxieties about my house aside. If she was indeed plotting something she would take her time. I think I'll set off back today though, a bit later on, and forego my last booked night. Not much point staying here for the sake of it and traveling up early tomorrow morning. I'll be able to have the full Friday at home this way.

Friday 17th September

I spent the whole drive back thinking about her. Thinking about her innocence. She is not 'savvy' nor 'streetwise'. She is naïve to this world and that is partly what makes her so wonderful. She can be childlike, *she can be happy*. All I could feel was how much I wanted her back with me and how much I want to spend my life with her and fulfil my, our dreams, and our life together in our cottage. The trip taught me how much I loved our trip together versus how much more empty every trip without her will be. I need to win her back and I spent the journey plotting all my next moves to have her back by my side. I could concentrate on removing obstacles, the knights and the bishops and the rooks or I could simply play to trap the queen. It works best if I do both, but the queen is the prize.

I am glad to be home on Friday, before the weekend. I did something rather odd today. I walked to the school at school time just to see all the Mums, Dads and children busy walking and skipping and talking and just being generally boisterous and active. It was quite a joy. I tried to just walk on by and not stare or dwell or anything as I don't want anyone thinking I am some sort of oddball. I thought that if I could plan my route carefully, I could do this every morning, just to give myself a bit of a lift, a bit of joy to see all those enthusiastic, energetic faces that haven't yet been soured or wrinkled by life. Their innocence seems to have no bounds, and it gives me a nice feeling just to feel a part of the hubbub. I know I am an outsider but it's nice just to be near.

I didn't see my car cleaning friend and I don't even know if this is the school he goes to, but I'll look out for him as it would be nice to see him again.

Saturday 18th September

I've inspected every inch of my property. Nothing has moved an inch. I am trying not to disturb anything or look like I am 'in' just in case she and her co-conspirator make their move, make a move. It is easy to live stealthily in one's own house and I am using the time to work out what next to do with her and what to do about Tom and this son of hers.

The spare bin is just as it was. I am to going get away with it, aren't I? *What fun.*

Sunday 19th September

Still nothing at all, nothing to see and nothing to do. With Tom I need to shatter the illusion somehow, with the son I need to lever their lack of relationship over the years. I need to break the fragile trust that exists. They hardly know each other. Divide and conquer. Somehow I'll look to find dirt and expose him. Real dirt or made up dirt, either is good for me. Then she'll have no choice but to run back into my arms. When she is the only piece left on that side of the board, she will want to join the winning side. She will see it is either that or checkmate. That is how I'll go about this. I felt pleased as I retired to bed, smug almost.

Monday 20th September

Her time is up. She did nothing, or nothing I can yet see or understand. Maybe this is all just a game of chess to her or maybe her son, or even worse, slimy Tom is now pulling her strings. *Ok darling, you win this time but that was just a battle, not the war.*

Do I text her now to say I'm back or what? What do I do now? I'm no clearer than before I left. Let's work out the detail of the plan.

Tuesday 21st September

I remembered this morning that I had resolved to go and see my Dad's grave and didn't and so I decided to go and see him today. I say 'him' but he's not really there is he and probably his remains are no longer under that piece of ground. Graves are for the living, not for the dead. They are there for those of us that remain so that we can feel better about permanence and about our ability for people not to forget us after we are gone. It's a tradition no doubt started by someone who was incredibly insecure or maybe one of those people that thought god was the sun. That was a perfectly rational thought once. How long before all of this other modern guff is seen as irrational and ridiculous. Not long, I hope.

But then, once I was there, I sat and I pondered and I thought about him. I did somehow, feel closer to him. I actually spoke out loud to him. So there did seem to be some sort of psychological trick going on somewhere and I thought about how this must bring comfort to many people. People who had been left behind by their soul mate perhaps. That must be terribly difficult.

It's been such a very long time since I saw my Dad. Time pushes him further and further away as I can only rely on my memories now. Everyone is so digital now that soon no one will ever really die, they just won't post anything new anymore. I miss him, I miss someone in my corner. I mostly miss the idea of him, I think.

Wednesday 22nd September

It occurred to me today that people have 'affairs' or transgressions and indiscretions in their lives all of the time. I remember such shenanigans being quite commonplace at work and indeed, it seemed ever more commonplace over time. I've never once thought about such a thing. Even when my marriage was at its most dull and irritating, I never considered that sleeping with another woman would be any sort of answer to any sort of question. Why do people do that? Is it the secrecy, their ego, just because they can or is it something else altogether? Is it fun, thrilling? And how do they do it, how do you go about setting up secret liaisons with someone regularly whilst trying never to be caught? How does it all start? It all must be terrifically exhausting.

Thursday 23rd September

We are all responsible, whether we like it or not. We cannot live in isolation from others. We are cohabiting this space and so we must all play our part. You wouldn't believe this to be true if you just watched any news bulletin the television can offer. Our televisions are bought and sold in more ways than one.

Friday 24th September

We humans have a skill that seems rarely talked about. We seem to be able to sense, whether through glass or even when the other person is behind us, when somebody else is looking directly at us. Look at someone in the eye, or just stare at the back of someone's head and they will respond, they will look back at you. What is that called, is it even a thing? It is definitely something though. It must be a defence against possible attack, an instinct for danger. It's underused and under talked about. I've never heard anyone talk about it.

Saturday 25th September

I sat and did my tax return today, how careless of me to allow it to go on this long without concluding the matter. I input all the required data and then had the extra pleasure of knowing, that if I do not work again in this tax year, I will be due another rebate next year as well. I am owed £229.86, which was a little bit less than I had calculated on my own spreadsheet, but there you go. Pretty close. I am already ready to do this again next year and I will try to ensure my calculation is a little more accurate next time.

Sunday 26th September

I decided today to go to the local library. I used to do it all the time but more recently much less so as everything is now so accessible on the internet. It was a long shot, but I wondered if I could find anything out about the father of her son. There just might have been some scandal at the time, given her age, and I might be able to establish who the father is. I really enjoyed spending time there. Some of the staff were the same as I remembered and they seemed to half remember me. Sadly, there were very few other patrons and nobody who looked remotely younger than me. The staff were so helpful and maybe a touch intrigued as to why I wanted to look at the microfiche from a certain period of time. I wondered, at one point, if their interest was something to do with a book I never returned. Thankfully not. I didn't let on what I was up to. It was needle in a haystack stuff but to my surprise there was indeed an article that explained how a local girl of just fifteen had given birth and that she would not reveal who the father was. But she must know. If she wouldn't reveal it at the time, he could be way older, or maybe the same age, but my guess was that she was hiding the truth for a reason. Protecting him and his identity must have been to serve a purpose. Now I have the date of birth perhaps there is more I can find out, more records I can check. *I am a sleuth, I will dig up the truth.*

Monday 27th September

Birth certificates are a matter of public record and so it was easy to get hold of that information but it didn't reveal anything new to me. I have started to think he was a little bastard and now I have the proof. I've poked around wherever I can think of but to no avail. I fear I might have hit a brick wall and the one person who can furnish me with the truth is the girl least likely to.

Tuesday 28th September

An uneventful day today in many ways. I tried to think clearly and so I did some gardening whilst there was still enough autumn sun. It was fresh and cold but the sun fooled me into staying outdoors. The peace and drinking plenty of water gave me the serenity to allow me to think through my next steps clearly. I enjoyed my day and my solitude. The birdsong in the garden was a joy. Just me and nature today. Maybe, that's how I prefer it now.

Wednesday 29th September

I received a surprise knock at the door today. The surprise was two-fold. Firstly, it gave me something of a start and secondly, as I peered through the small glass section to see who it was before I opened it, and upon my restricted examination, I thought it might be her son. But why? *Does he even know who his father is?*

I opened the door with some sense of surprise and not an insignificant amount of trepidation. 'Can I come in?' he said. I quickly considered the danger I might be in and any physical threat he posed but I decided the conversation was worth the risk and I felt, despite his assertive nature, that he wasn't out of control or here to start a fight. He was certainly physically stronger than me, plus he has youth on his side.

At first, he tried to warn me off. He is somewhat inarticulate and so it was hard to follow him. He said I had been poking around in business that was not my concern. *Interesting.* He told me to stop. Whilst I still wasn't sure quite what he was driving at, the picture was becoming clearer. This was all to do with his father. The man who had decided, before he was even born, that he wanted nothing to do with him. *Ouch.*

He kept asking me what business it was of mine. I needed to tread carefully. I didn't want to over tease him or set off any rage within him. In the end, I didn't really need to say anything as he just kept on talking all by himself.

Then he said something about the truth hurting and I had no idea what he meant by that, but I assumed he was hurting at the rejection of one of his parents. Well, both initially.

He then started to reveal his truth, the truth. It was a much older man. Someone of standing in the community. She insisted on keeping the baby after he had demanded she terminate it. *Ouch again.* In the end he had given her a financial settlement to keep his name out of things. He had then shown no apparent interest in the child and offered nothing more. He wiped his hands clean of the whole thing, like some sort of business deal. He never even saw him. *This must hurt in the deepest of places.*

I could visibly see, without much effort, just how hard this was for him to talk about and he struggled to keep his composure and assertion throughout. He didn't want to play the victim, he had come to tell me to back off and I did begrudgingly admire his fortitude. He softened a touch and said he understood my curiosity but my poking around could do no good now, it could only stir things up, things that had been settled for a long time. He said if both he and her could leave this well alone for all this time then I should be able to as well. He gained some strength back as he gave me this advice.

He then turned again somewhat. He got angry and he said 'You don't even want to know. You don't even want to know anymore' and then he looked at me with forceful piercing eyes and he left. I had hardly spoken and we certainly didn't seem to agree anything. It was a bizarre experience and it did ruffle my feathers. I tried to act cool but inside I felt the upset.

I couldn't sleep that night as his words, the whole episode, just played around in my head. I felt like there was something more to this, something significant. A long-buried secret and that is what made me feel like pursuing it further. But what would I gain from unearthing this and what might I lose along the way? I tried to convince myself to leave this well alone, to focus on winning her back and then, one day, she would tell me. But I felt conflicted.

Thursday 30th September

This morning I was awake at 4.15am. I still have no idea why my brain, the same brain that needs sleep, decides to wake me up. It makes no sense. I had a look at my phone and I had received a text from her at 2.23am. 'We need to talk. Can I come round later today?' *So serious and no kiss.* Clearly a reaction to his visit. She must have known he had visited. Did she send him? I assumed she meant after work, her work, but no, she wanted to come round first thing and by 7.15am she was here and we were drinking coffee. I had that horrible anticipatory feeling you get just before you get one of life's bombshells, that type that you don't easily come back from. I think this was because she insisted on coming round so early, upsetting her own routine so it was clearly more important than work. I was shaking as she arrived and she was pulling the exact face I didn't want to see. I tried to look composed but I had so many emotions coursing through my veins. I think it was the sheer oddity of everything that was upsetting my natural rhythm.

We sat and she asked how yesterday had gone with her son. She said he struggles with his emotions and in particular the thought that his own father wanted nothing to do with him. I said I understood and told her just how important a figure my father was in my young life and then she grimaced, held her stomach and started to cry.

She revealed to me who the father was. I thought it was a sick joke. It must be. It was my Dad. My Dad is his Dad. He had been tutoring her privately and the details she gave were too precise to be made up. She wouldn't be capable of lying like this and expressing all this pain and her very nature wouldn't have ever allowed her to imagine this up or tell me this if it wasn't the honest truth. Her pain was now insignificant to mine. I threw up. He paid her off. He didn't want the family scandal. She said my mother knew all about it. She said she thought my sister knew nothing of it. She said she didn't realise I was his son when we got together as my surname is relatively common. It never crossed her mind. I don't have any pictures of him up so she never made the connection. But clearly one day she had. Exactly when?

My Dad. The last bastion of the strength I have. My blood, my only true mentor and hero had done this. I don't know who or what I am now. I have been stripped of my identity, stripped as painfully as if the very skin of my back had been peeled off by a blunt knife. My flagpole disintegrated and me, the flag is now just at the mercy of the wind with nothing to cling to, nothing to hold me in place. I was totally confused as to what this means to her son and me. *Is he related to me? He must be.* My Dad has spoiled any chance of a future relationship with the only woman I have ever truly loved. *I think.*

Eventually she left. I was numb, in shock. She was the same. Just when we needed each other, we parted. I sat at the table and thought about drinking some whisky. That's not something I do but I needed numbness and quickly. I think I sat there for hours, on the floor, just staring at the wall with my mouth wide open. I think I eventually just passed out.

Later, as I laid in bed, I thought about all the questions I wished I had asked her but mainly all I could consider was exactly when was it that she had realised he was my Dad.

Friday 1st October

I got up, but I hadn't really slept.

The first of the month always has the air of a fresh start for me but not today. I could think of nothing much and I couldn't even think of texting her. I just played with my phone. I was idly scanning through my phone when I inadvertently came across a tracker app that has been installed without my knowledge. The suspect list has but one name on it. *How dare you!*

She has some explaining to do. My focus returned. What concerned me most was just how long the tracker has been on there and how far back in time my movements have been traceable? This could be of significance, but maybe less so if she hasn't told anybody else or really been keeping tabs on me at critical times. I felt a touch better. She is hardly the type. It might explain her approach to me recently though, the distance between us. But then was that all to do with my Dad? My mind is whirring. How does all of this now fit together? I need to take some action, I felt the need to do something but I needed to calm down and plan things carefully. I needed to get some control back. *Full control.*

Saturday 2nd October

I distracted myself a little today as I had worked out a basic plan to use the money I found. I took one of the fifty pound notes to the local bookmakers. I had never placed a bet before in my life so I had to watch others do it and found it to be an easy task. I could make it look like it was something I did regularly. The odds system is very basic maths and so I placed fifty pounds on the favourite. It lost but if I keep doing that, I'm sure I'll convert the money and be at least, maybe five grand up, with cleaner notes. Fifty pounds on the favourite as often as I dare. It's a stroke of genius. I feel like I am money laundering and it's exciting. No trail at all though and great fun. When it's done, I'll give the clean money to charity. I'll have to do this sparingly and not too often and I'll have to use different bookmakers. I might need to travel and if so, I'll deduct my expenses from the total. I'll also need to be careful regarding my appearance as they have CCTV all over the place as I imagine they are susceptible to armed robberies more than most. I might stand out a bit though as the other customers gave me the impression that they basically live there. They smell the same as the shop. They also seemed to place very small bets but very often. Fifty pence often. Maybe I can do research on horses and make this fun. It can be a new hobby, just until all the notes I found are swapped.

The other thing I did today, which I might not repeat, was to give a homeless lady one of the fifty pound notes. I couldn't stop to take any thanks as I needed to avoid her really seeing my face but the moment was just long enough for me to see hers when she realised what it was and, to be honest, it gave me a really warm, lovely feeling. It felt just like I imagined, like a modern day Robin Hood. I needed to feel like I had done some good today, perhaps even to feel some element of comradeship. It fully sank in today that my life is now destined to be a singular one, that whilst I could seek some more answers, or more information, there seemed little to no possibility of me being a part of her life again and nothing inside of me wanted to be a part of his.

Sunday 3rd October

I invited her round for tea today. We are in touch a little bit more regularly now but maybe only because of the need to talk things through. She continues to be ever more distant, yet somehow compassionate. She is, and has always been though, an incredibly poor liar. Her neck goes all red and blotchy and her speech is broken and high pitched. *A poker player she is not.* I happened, in all innocence, to ask her if she had ever heard of said tracker and at that point she crumbled instantly and looked at the floor. *Guilty as charged.* I do not like someone else exercising such control over me without my consent. *What sort of thought process led her to putting this on my phone?* What I really needed to know was how long it has been on there. She claimed to know nothing of it. A total lie. I played along for there is nothing to be gained at this point by forcing her away. I deleted it in front of her eyes, all innocently. I might have to gamble that it was a recent thing or something she didn't look at too often, or just when I didn't want her to. What are the odds of her being able to place me in situations I need to keep clandestine. There's not much I can really do about it now anyway. I've changed my phone passcode now too. There are only really two situations I needed her to not see.

The most crucial question I asked her was when she had twigged that I was the son of the monster in her life. She choked to speak of my father, she said at the time she was infatuated by him, that she had played a role in them coming together. I asked if he knew full well she was fifteen. She nodded. *How could she offer him any kind of defence?* I tried to pull her back to my point. *When did she realise he was my Dad?* She said not until recently. *A poker player she is not.*

Monday 4th October

When people say 'Oh, it's a long story' it is very rarely a long story, it is more the case that they just can't be bothered to take two minutes to explain something. They are bored of themselves and everything has to be so piecemeal and so instant nowadays that to take a few minutes to explain something is now seemingly beyond the wit of man.

I regained my focus a little today. I had been distracted by my father's terrible behaviour. It was incomprehensible to me and I didn't know if it had shattered his standing in my mind. Was it all a mistake? Everyone makes mistake. Could I forgive him? Were they in love or did he prey on under age girls? Was she the only one? Did he indeed offer private tuition to harvest such opportunities? I was putting myself through the mill with no way of ever coming out the other side with any clarity. How could he pay her off and never want to see his own son? Nobody knows the answers to this but him and, to some degree, maybe her. My head cleared and I knew the tracker could be vital in terms of what she, or anyone she might have spoken to, including the police, knew. But again, this was out of my control. She would hardly tell me if I could be incriminated.

The tension was too much. *Too much.*

I tried distracting myself with my new hobby but my horse lost again today and my heart wasn't in it so I feel like I am simply giving my find to local bookmakers. Betting on horses is such a mugs game and how could anybody not see it. The cashier doesn't win, the customer doesn't win, the winner is the corporation, the company. *How very 21st century I thought.* This didn't seem to serve my intention at all and clearly, I was not serving any valiant purpose whatsoever. I'll stick with the plan for now but I might need to reconsider.

Tuesday 5th October

I went round to her house this evening uninvited. She was in, she was alone and I essentially pushed my way in and closed the door behind me. I felt myself boiling over but couldn't calm my thoughts enough not to turn up. It was a mistake and one I now need to somehow conceal or sort. As soon as I arrived, I could feel my emotions, my anger, taking over. She tells me nothing, she is wary of me in some way and I felt like she was taking me for a fool. *She put a tracker on my phone and I don't even know when!* As she talked of work and general pleasantries, I cut her off mid-sentence and asked 'When did you put the tracker on my phone?' She could see I looked angry and that I was full of intent. 'When!' I repeated. She froze with kettle in hand. She literally froze on the spot. She looked weak but my anger pushed me to force my advantage and not to see how I might be hurting her. I smashed a cup on the floor. 'When?' I repeated. 'I do not want to ask again!'. She came back to life and was shaking all over. 'Mid-May' she said. My mind processed this new and crucial information in the best way it could. A lot to recount. The information was both worrying and not specific enough in equal measure. I tried to calm down and I apologised, but I knew I had made things worse, but we are way past the point of return now. With that in mind I concentrated on my survival. 'Sit down' I said. 'I want to know exactly when'. She looked incredibly scared, as if she feared for her life. She reached for her phone, but I forcibly snatched it off her. She said she was just trying to look at her calendar. 'Tell me when, tell me why, tell me what prompted you or I swear.....' She interrupted with the news I did not want. She had put the tracker on my phone in Mid-May, the night, as she described it, when I moved my car late in the evening without any mention or apparent need. I knew instantly which night she meant. I asked her how often she looked at it and what she knew of my whereabouts. She must have known what I was driving at. She said she rarely looked and knew nothing. 'Liar!' I shouted, 'Tell me what you know!' with as big a physical threat as I could muster. She cried and spluttered that she didn't know anything. 'Have you shared any information with anyone else?' I asked. This could only mean her son and the police. I was controlled but as menacing as I could possibly be. I was fully in charge by now, I felt better. She said 'no' and then I insisted she unlock her phone. She wailed and resisted but she eventually had no choice. I didn't want to physically hurt her as it would leave evidence, but I wondered, for the first time, if I now really needed her out of the way for good.

Once in her phone the genie leapt out of the bottle. Screen shots of my location. She kept texts with my dead sister, texts from former colleagues, texts even with James. And the texts with her son were a revelation too. Did she know I was at Ms Hinchcliffe's that night? There is a conspiracy against me, a cabal no less. Notes of her thoughts and suspicions. Texts with Tom, her supposed boss. *Oh, how familiar you two now are, what a surprise.* James claiming he saw me on the street near her ex boyfriends on the actual day. The truth spilled out into my eyes. It destroyed any last remnants of love for her and instantly galvanised my spirit. *I know what I have to do.*

'I'm sorry' I said, 'I'm, of course, going to have to keep this. And, before I leave, I think we need a chat about what you are going to do next'

Of course, I was far from clear about what my plan should be, but it felt too risky to just leave. So, I sat there all night, just thinking. She said nothing. Did she feel like a prisoner in her own home? Did she know what I was capable of? How much of all my actions did she know? Who has she told and exactly what has she said? Has she been talking to the police?

Insults were so easily thrown. Nasty language either way. Taunts even about what my Dad could have seen in her and how she must have been a young slut. I don't even know if I meant a word of it. Was I just lashing out? Was I just hurting and scared? Like a piece of balsa wood, we snapped and I knew that we could never be the same again. The look between us was hate. This was now survival, not reconciliation.

At one point she tried to throw a verbal punch. She said she knew I has called her new employer to try and spread lies about her to try and get them to retract their offer. *A new chapter is born, no going back after this.* She cowered as she delivered the final word. My instinct was to deny this as she cannot possibly have known it was me that made the call. But, instead I said 'That's the least I am capable of, the least of your worries'. Her meek voice and weak body was no match for me. I saw the fear in her eyes. A fear I found useful. She said 'Like father, like son', the ultimate insult and I was more stunned than angry but of course I threw back the insult with interest. Yet there was a strange logic in this clumsiest of lines. I refocused. I asked, What sort of fifteen year old entraps an old man. I didn't wait for nor want a reply. The answer I gave to my own question was the worst insult I have ever thrown at anyone. *Why would I even consider defending him and his honour?* Because I didn't want to lose him, the only constant I have ever had and I knew she was now long gone.

Yes, this was a long night and one where survival instincts were far more important than sleep. I had to think my way out of this and here was a unique opportunity that might not return.

Wednesday 6th October

I awoke and enjoyed that second or two we all get before our lives and brains kick back in again. She was asleep on the chair. It was

4.15am. *What on earth am I doing?* For now, I should destroy this phone, offer apologies and some trust and work it out from there. The phone has hard evidence, her word holds no water. I needed some control here, but I cannot keep her prisoner. *That's the wrong play.*

I waited until 5.30am and then I made her a coffee. I woke her up and saw her too enjoy that priceless first moment and then I saw her face as mine registered in her eyes. *How on earth did we get here my darling?* I gave her the coffee. I apologised as sincerely as I could, I told her she needed to get ready for work. I explained I was still in shock. She seemed as if she believed me, she seemed surprised, relieved even, until I said that I would, of course, need to keep hold of her phone. I needed to do research into how to ensure the phone is wiped from everything including the cloud. I could leave no trace.

As she left for work, I left too. She locked the door and stumbled to the bus stop. She didn't want a lift from me, *as if she would.*

I went home and read then deleted everything she had on her phone except her contacts. She has me at the location of her ex-boyfriend on the critical day. But nothing of me inside the actual house as far as I could see. Not good, but not totally disastrous. Still relatively damning though and enough to bring about very uncomfortable questions I would rather not face. I couldn't see anything suggesting I was at Ms Hinchcliffe's that day. I am perhaps saved by the sheer obviousness of me taking action against her. Everything could still point to me though I was confused. What if she had shared and then deleted stuff? Never let your enemy know what you are not prepared to do. But I can only contain, not solve.

I am a mess.

I stored the numbers of her contacts in my phone too. I tried, with research, to delete everything but I couldn't convince myself of wiping it fully clean. I feared the convenience of the modern day back-up, the cloud, and what have you.

Thursday 7th October

I went round to return her phone to her but there was nobody in. *Where is she?* I have no way of telling, nor contacting her at the moment and that is not good, not satisfactory at all. She must be at her sons, she must be.

Friday 8th October

I stayed at home today as if I somehow needed to guard my castle. It was a trick of the mind I didn't appreciate as I ended up like some sort of caged tiger, just pacing up and down, waiting for something to happen. *Waiting for what to happen?* I awaited a move whilst not making a move. I tried to induce contact and increase understanding. *By doing what exactly?* Should I go round again? What should I do? I felt like I couldn't go out for fear of missing something. *Missing what exactly?*

I reconciled that time had passed. The police hadn't come for me and the more time that passed, the less likely that would be. Could I strike some sort of deal with her? Did I need to? I still have no idea what she knows really.

This was not a good day for me. My brain continues to try to calculate how I am related to her son. I think I am his half-brother? The thought repulses me in every way. How come he is so thick and inarticulate. I want nothing more to do with him. My Dad was right. She trapped him, he was stuck and so he thought his way out. He probably saw the baby, the little bastard and realised he had nothing he wanted from it or to give to it. He did the decent thing and gave her money to ensure she'd be okay.

How I feel about her, I do not really know.

Saturday 9th October

I decided to go round to hers again today. I knocked and knocked on the door, but nobody answered, and it looked to me like the house might have been empty for a few days. It had that cold feel about it and the same lighting as last time when she had left it empty. *Won't you ever learn?* I posted her phone through the letter box in a padded envelope having checked and checked again as much as I could that I had done everything I could to wipe off anything meaningful against me both inside and on the outside of the phone. There was no harm in giving it back. Perhaps more harm in having it with me. Where are you and what are you thinking, who have you spoken to and what have you said? I need to be able to at least talk to you to get a handle on this situation. Where could she be? Back with the bastard son, no doubt.

Sunday 10th October

She must be with her son. She must be. That's the only location that makes any sense. She doesn't really have anyone else and they have a lot to discuss, and much of it could only galvanise them. I am starting to think they somehow deserve each other. Anyway, who else would take her in and, crucially, who else would she ask? I don't have much to go on but I must be able to track him down somehow.

She has lived with all that shame for so long. Plus the added weight of her not bringing up her own son. I wonder what she did with Dad's money? She has had it tough and she still found a way to absorb some of the blame when we spoke.

I tried to find ways to track him down, but I've nothing much to go on and the tracker is now useless as the now wiped phone is just sitting on her doormat anyway. I can actually call him as I have his number from her phone. I am going to need to be cunning as he will be very much on guard. *How to approach such a challenge?*

Monday 11th October

A stroke of luck today as I drove to her house only to see her inside it. Her son was waiting outside for her in his car. He was looking around and seemed a tad nervous. I called him whilst withholding my number and sure enough, on cue, he answered the call. *Just so you know, I thought.* I of course, immediately hung up but now I can follow him to his home, to her temporary home. As easy as pie, I followed them, very carefully, so now I know where she is staying, where the bastard lives.

Tuesday 12th October

I drove to his house again today. It looks as if he is giving her lifts to work and maybe back again. My brain is not working as I had forgotten I could have just tracked her from work. I wonder what he does for a living? How can I get to her and keep him out of the way? I called her phone, again withholding my number but no answer, just voicemail. So, I do not know whether she is using that phone at all, has it with her even, or is using an entirely different number. I am getting closer though. I do wonder sometimes what her son thinks of me and of Dad, *our Dad.* That thought sickens me to my core. Does he want to get to know me? He's only ever heard her side of the story.

Wednesday 13th October

I looked at my finances today and it seems I am spending money at a rate faster than I anticipated. It is not easy to adjust not having money coming in, especially given my saving nature. I suppose this is how it works, this is the system. Save up through working and then spend it as you get older. It would be easier to plan if we all knew when we were going to die. I suppose I could take control of that, but few do, they all just leave it to fate, to disease or whatever. I don't want to run out but equally I don't want to die with a pile of cash in the bank. Plus, my inheritance is due soon, I hope. I must check in with the solicitor and nudge him along. Time is money.

Thursday 14th October

I must see the doctor tomorrow. I felt dizzy and faint again today. You can't book an appointment the day before. 'Why not?' I asked, but the answer, as with most conversations in modern life, was not an answer to my question but just a repeat of the policy. 'That's not what I asked' I said. Call in the morning at eight she said. That's my only option, to fight with everyone else to see a GP for a few minutes. Surely, they can see I am due some time. I've never bothered them with anything for years.

Friday 15th October

I did get an appointment quite easily in the end. A Dr McCaffrey will see me. Like everyone, he seemed so young. He said there was nothing wrong with me and he asked if I had been having a stressful time recently. *Well, where does one start with that question?* He asked me what I did for a living and I stumbled to answer. *I really should have this prepared better by now.* I said I left my job at the end of July, but I seemed to say it with some unintentional shame. Anyway, he said he would check my bloods and that if I didn't hear anything back, that meant I was okay. What a strange system, so I asked how long is it before I can be sure I won't hear anything and he said maybe 5-7 days. When I asked whether he meant working days or calendar days he gave me a funny, knowing look over his glasses and just said that if I get worse to come back. *Well, it's your stupid system.* If I need to see a consultant, I'll pay for one privately to speed things along. I'd have used the health cover from work, but I obviously don't have that now and never considered that I ought to take out an alternative policy. How unusually remiss of me. Hopefully it is just nothing though.

With some irony, on my return home I twisted my ankle quite badly. I just misjudged the step. That got me thinking, if I did need ever need to stay in hospital, or ever got rushed to hospital, I think only my darling would visit me, nobody else. *She would come, wouldn't she? There is no chance now.*

It's the ones who keep in touch, the ones who ask you how you are without a prompt. They are the ones worth bothering with. There aren't that many, but they are precious.

Saturday 16th October

It was all too much today. I think the doctor's appointment might have affected me. I went to her son's house. I knocked on the door. As bold as brass and just like that, without very much planning, more on instinct. My ankle throbbing didn't help my mood at all. She has been ignoring my calls so what choice did I have? He came to the door. Of course he did. I know he is physically bigger than me but by no means my intellectual equal. I assessed that in about five seconds the other day, when he came to visit me. I asked him to give us some space, some time together. His indignation was all too apparent. He clearly thinks I am some sort of ogre, some sort of threat. I saw her behind him. I pleaded her just to speak to me, to hear me out for a few minutes. She eventually agreed. I was let in. I stayed calm. Control is everything. *This is my game, so my rules.* We talked but she was so closed off from me, she looked at me only sideways and as if I was an actual monster of some sort. *How have we come to this?* I pleaded again for us to have some sort of relationship, some sort of chance to find a path back to our happiness and to our cottage in Devon or Cornwall or anywhere. *I don't even want that anymore.* I only really wanted her on side for what might be a tricky road in the next few months. I even suggested the three of us could talk, could iron things out and at least find some civility. *I felt sick.* I said we were all victims and so we could somehow stick together. *This was stretching even my acting skills.* These thoughts were sickening to me and the words very nearly made me vomit. I looked at him to try and see what he was thinking and although I never left his sight I got nothing but cold rejection from his eyes, hate even. *I am not the villain here.* He stood, cross armed, stalking me and asserting some sort of physical authority. *But I am in charge here Sonny.* I asked her if she had picked up her phone after I had posted it back to her and she said yes, but that she now has a new one. Her voice tailed off to nothing as she said it. I asked for the number, and she just shook her head with some sort of embarrassment and sorrow. She hid her face as best she could. I knew at that point that my chances of any sort of alliance or assistance were next to, if not absolutely, zero. My anger started to grow. The fire inside. Who does she think she is, watching me come round here and beg for her forgiveness? How special does she actually think she is? I could find another ten of her easily. I kept my outward cool and asked if I might have a tea or a water. He stupidly went into the kitchen and put the kettle on. He felt he had made some sort of assessment of me and established a control. *But I am in charge here Sonny, you little bastard.* Then, under my breath, I let her know what I really thought. Shacked up with her estranged son in his dirty little house. I told her I knew everything about her, everything, and that I could bring her down in an instant. I told her that I know just how fragile she is. That I could drop her in it with the police through an odd white lie. She started to stand up, possibly getting ready to shout but I was up and on her faster. I held her by the shoulders, hard, and felt the urge to grasp her throat. It was hard to resist but I couldn't leave a mark. I told her she had better say nothing because she knew nothing and that if she did it would affect her in ways she could never dream of. I saw the fear, I saw the panic. *I was winning.* I heard him coming back so I sat back down and put my fingers to my lips to indicate to her that she had better not say anything. But she found a new bravery that I wasn't prepared for. She ran to him, knocking over the drinks she told him I had threatened her. I played innocent, 'She's mad' I said. *I can act.* He looked confused. *You see, I know he doesn't really know her that well at all does he.* I stood up and reached for my coat trying to take advantage of the doubt. I volunteered to leave and was very happy to do so whilst there was still considerable confusion. All he could see was a reasonable man. As I left, I smiled. A victory. But then I felt a tap on the shoulder, I turned around and he punched me across the jaw. The pain was instant and I was knocked over, shocked and I pulled a small table in the hall with me as I went. He looked unsure so I said, very calmly 'Why did you do that?' He was breathing heavily but then, my anger, my frustration, the pain and embarrassment got the better of me and I said 'The silly bitch doesn't deserve to be defended and least not by a little bastard like you'. I continued to put the knife in, 'Neither of your parents could bear to look at you, never mind raise you.'. He instantly moved to kick me but I winced as he drew his foot back and he withdrew. I stood up. 'The police will be hearing about this assault' I said. They looked at each other. Like me, they were making this up as they went along. This was a lie as I don't want to speak to them ever again and then I threw in 'You know that she is a killer don't you. Yes, she torched her ex-boyfriends house and murdered him. She was arrested. I bet she didn't tell you about that!'. This seemed to trigger her like a lit firework. She screamed, 'That's not true, it was him and he killed his sister and probably his mother too and next, I think he is going to kill me'. I had never seen her look like this. It was most unattractive and unbecoming, not ladylike at all. The son looked confused, which was fair enough. 'You of all people should know what she is capable of, how cold she can be, I mean, who would leave their own baby?' He was still breathing heavily and looking to somehow express his emotions physically, but he seemed to have no idea what to do. *I was particularly cruel.*

'She is bonkers, mental beyond repair, believe what you like but the police will nail her eventually and she'll leave you all over again then' I said and I left feeling my split lip. I could feel the swelling starting to grow already. I still felt anger above all else. My final glance at her was meant to convey that this was a long way from over. I needed her to feel fear to help protect myself.

As I made it back to my car, I tried to process all that had happened. I knew instinctively that there were some wins but maybe bigger losses and the gravity of my potential situation was clearer. I need to move to survival mode now and remove any thoughts of being with her ever again. Plus, she thinks I killed my sister, which I certainly did not. Well not in the way she thinks anyway.

Sunday 17th October

I toyed with the idea of sending an anonymous letter into her work. Some sort of continued smear campaign. Everyone believes there is no smoke without fire and so if I keep going, I am sure I would get some traction eventually. Something vague and menacing along the lines of 'She isn't who you think she is' and the like. Something to cause her distress, to unnerve the employer and make them suspicious and check. Something to blot her copybook and something to let her know I am still here and threatening. Something they can't trace back to me. It feels like a good idea but not fully and properly formed. Maybe it can become a campaign. That's something I might enjoy. I need to think it through though and come up with a more pointed and effective idea.

Monday 18th October

I sat at home today and mainly pondered. I tried listening to music but couldn't settle. I tried to read, but again, I couldn't settle. Even doing housework or going for a walk couldn't really help me be at ease with myself. No television or film would do. So eventually I just sat, tried to meditate, and then fell asleep. I awoke around 2pm, with literally nothing to do and my sleep-soaked brain invited me to think about prison for a while. To be subjected to prison would be of no benefit to the system or to me. I don't want to live among criminals. I would have to make bad choices simply to survive. I'd want to serve out my sentence as peacefully as possible, but I imagine the environment would simply not allow this. I am not physically intimidating and so my ethical code would face dilemmas and challenges it could not simply ignore. My need to navigate and survive without inducing any physical harm might force me to choose a gang that I would rather not be part of. Then I might have to prove myself to my gang in ways I'd rather not. I'd possibly have to subscribe to beliefs I do not have. I would need to join 'a side'. All of this might mean that, against my plan, I might end up in trouble as I try to prove myself to my gang by having to hurt someone in another gang with whom I have absolutely no quarrel. My time in prison might actually therefore increase and I might not come out the man that went in. I'd be a new, worse version of me, no doubt bitter and vengeful and ready to settle the score. You see, it would be no good for anyone and certainly no good for me. That's what I imagine prison to be because that, for those of us lucky enough not to be in prison, is the same scenario we face in our daily lives. Politicians seek power and immediate gain as the game is election and re-election not long-term vision and planning. The CEO tries to increase his bonus and the dividend pay-out year on year rather than steering the ship for the good of the world or the planet. Lawyers defend the guilty, and maybe win, for their fee. The best ones are available to the highest bidder, not the ones with the strongest case. These are the rules of the game for us all, for now at least. I don't want to go to prison though *life is a prison*.

I have no idea what sentence I would get as I have no idea what the charges would actually be.

Tuesday 19th October

I looked at my will today with a view to amending it. I have been remiss in leaving it this long. The sole beneficiary of my estate is my dead wife. I scoffed out loud when I saw that. I did hit me quite hard that, whilst I know I need to amend it, I don't really have a new beneficiary to insert. Of course, there is only one person I would want to have my money but then that made me think all my worth would end up in the pocket of her estranged son and that didn't feel right. Would Dad approve? In fact, it felt downright weird. I think I'll leave it to charity. I mean, what do I care, I won't be here will I.

Wednesday 20th October

Do I still love her deep down? If so, I need to admit that and deal with it as there are now bigger games to play and there is no chance of us reconciling. None.

Thursday 21st October

I've realised that as I walk, and because my route is now so regular, I see much the same people every day. The old man with the stick and the big teeth, still full of life and always says 'Hiya Kidda' unnecessarily loudly. He is so old he regards me as a youngster. The little woman with the cap who always says hello as if she shouldn't, as if she is not quite worthy of anybody else's attention. The wellington booted dog walker. Always prepared for the bad weather and with three always, over enthusiastic and rather large dogs and then there is the 'normal' woman. The woman who is in no way outstanding at all, her coat is off the peg, her height is average, her haircut short. She looks like nothingness itself. She is average in every way and barely noticeable, but we got to the stage where we actually said hello to each other often accompanied by a half-fake smile and an unconvincing nod of the head. In fact, the only thing I have actually noticed about her is how, in recent times, she has come to blank me, to ignore me, to look the other way almost purposefully as to ensure our gaze should not meet. She is nothing to me, not even does she have a cameo role in my life's movie but somehow, I've noticed her change in behaviour and I've noticed how I try not to try and think about it and consider what I might have done for her to decide not to nod or murmur hello anymore. What could I have done, why has she changed, why does this matter one smidgeon to me? Why do I consider it? Why, as she approaches do I wonder if she will, today, revert and acknowledge my existence. What is wrong with her?

Friday 22nd October

I stayed in all day today. I didn't venture out. I even cried a little once. I needed today, just to reset.

Saturday 23rd October

Saturday hasn't felt like Saturday for a long time so I decided to go to a new bookies with two of my fifty pound notes. I gave one away to a homeless chap with a dog. The look on his face was worth it and his excitement immediately passed to the dog. It felt good. I definitely picked the wrong bookmakers though as when I walked in, I felt like an intruder. Suspicion grew as I placed a crisp fifty pound note on the favourite of the very next race. I wanted to leave but they took my confidence and fifty pound stake as some kind of indication of information or knowledge and they all put money on the same horse too. Some of the customers winked at me and I suddenly felt that if the horse lost I might well struggle to leave. The thrill was quite amazing, it is a while since I have felt anything close to that. It won and I was given eighty three pounds and thirty three pence. The worst part of it was that she gave me my fifty pound note back. I could hardly ask for a different note. I left but the locals weren't happy, they wanted more of the same. I am sure one of them followed me for a bit so I walked through the shopping centre to lose him. I won't be going back there again in a hurry.

Sunday 24th October

I didn't venture out at all again today. I sat, I plotted and I considered next moves. I still don't feel composed, I still cannot see my path forward.

Monday 25th October

The postman shook me today. *That stiff letterbox.* It was such a waste of time and effort too as every letter was either junk mail or something I immediately shredded or recycled.

Tuesday 26th October

I decide today to do nothing further about Tom. I barely leave the house these days and it is too risky to do anything at all for such little reward. If he wants to get together with her and her little bastard son then he can. He can tell her how to raise a baby, how to change a nappy.

Wednesday 27th October

I did eventually venture out today. Just to pursue my favourite new hobby again. I am running out of bookmakers I can walk to though so I might have to start to drive to them soon. I prefer the local ones as that means I am giving to a local homeless person too. The thrill of giving someone who has so little, a crisp fifty pound note, is a joy unrivalled. It's a shame I can't stay and chat but I really cannot begin to build a reputation nor create a pattern as god knows where this money came from or who it belongs to. I imagine the police would like to track it down somehow and I have had more than enough of them and do not need anymore attention. When I looked at the horses a wise looking old man told me which one to pick. His eyes had an experienced look and his slight Irish accent captivated me momentarily. I put the fifty on and watched the race. It wasn't even near the front at any point. His confidence drained quickly and he hid behind his flat cap. As I left, I smiled as to how I had been hoodwinked by a man who clearly lives part time in a bookmakers. I made my way home.

Thursday 28th October

I stayed in bed all day today. I just didn't have a good enough reason to get up. I cannot recall ever doing this before in my whole life.

Friday 29th October

I went for my regular haircut today and the lady, Shona, who has been cutting my hair in exactly the same way for years, is no longer there. They were indeed more than sketchy about where she had gone but it certainly knocked me off my stride. Some young, tattooed woman who couldn't stop talking about herself and asking me personal questions had a go at it and I was far from pleased. *What do you do? What are you doing today? What are you doing for the weekend?* Please just shut up. Shona both understood what I wanted with my hair and what I wanted from our exchange. Competence and discretion. Do the job, I'll pay, with tip, and leave.

I was more than a little disconcerted about the whole thing but I still left a tip and my hair is fine. Do I look for Shona or do I get used to this single mother who just cannot stop talking? Why did this also have to change? I also had a nagging feeling that Shona might not indeed, be okay.

Saturday 30th October

I only have old photos now. They have more value as they were scarce and more difficult to attain. There are billions of images flying all over the world every second but they are not the same as the old, physical photos. They are to treasure and they are special. The modern world's craving for volume and ease has killed anything we might want to cherish. I have a particular one of my Dad that reminds me of how I used to see him, how he was to me. I love that old photo.

Sunday 31st October

The clocks change today. This never used to bother me but now it has caused me to break our calendar year up into two sections. Light and dark. Now we have five months of dark to face and it doesn't feel great. You can take advantage of the dark though. There are things that it allows you to do so much better, so much easier.

Something made me believe it would have been my sister's birthday today but then I realised I am a month early. Why do we think about dead people's birthdays and when does this stop? I mean, you don't hear anyone saying it would have been so and so's 148th birthday today, do you?

Nobody came to my door this evening in the name of Halloween. Another stupid tradition on its way out, I hope. Thank goodness for that. My door is there but knocks are really not welcomed. I did hold some hope out that my car washing friend might return and I had a crisp five pound note ready for him, just in case.

Monday 1st November

Every 1st of the month seems to have been a Monday this year. Everything is in order when those aspects of time align. Still no call from the premium bonds people and I might have to look to cash some in, in the not too distant future, if my inheritance takes much longer.

Tuesday 2nd November

I woke up to the most chilling of thoughts. She had never shown me the necklace, the one her grandmother had bequeathed to her. Now I understand her horror, her disgust. How could I make such an error? I only saw it as I stole it, never before.

What exactly do I do now?

Wednesday 3rd November

Today I contacted the police. I wish I had given myself just a little more space to plan but I decided that if I cannot have her then nobody else is going to have her and in prison, I knew, only I would offer to visit her. So she would be like a goldfish, or pet, to me. It might offer us a long road back to togetherness. I felt I had to act quickly. I told the police everything. I told them how she had been in touch with her boyfriend almost constantly and had deleted messages between them. I told them of the fights they had, both on the phone and face to face. How she had lied to them about being in his house. How he was intimidating but not overly bright. How he broke into her house to vandalise it. I told them how she confided in me that she was there again, at his house, on the day of the fire and that she had decided to dress up, as a man, in my clothes, to disguise herself. I reminded them that she said she was at my house all day yet nobody saw her or could substantiate that. I told them her lies could surely not have fooled them. I told them she was a deeply troubled individual and how she could not even cope with being made redundant, how I had become some kind of carer to her. How she had become increasingly irrational and wayward in her behaviour. I said I couldn't sleep and even though I loved her deeply my conscience was getting the better of me. I said that if she had done that to him then what else might she have done or what else might she be capable of. I said I was scared. My performance was superb. My tears, my shaking voice, my regret, the cathartic nature of my revealing of the truth, the release of this burden, my struggle to tell all. I didn't mention her abandoning her baby though at fifteen years old. That would have been too far, unfair and also pretty irrelevant. *My darling, I have some sorrow but given where we now are, this is for the best. You'll get a lighter sentence than me.*

Thursday 4th November

How do you get a job? It's so hard. How do you find a partner? It's so hard. The hard things are so easy to us now, so instant and attainable. Press a button and you have what you want. But there are those things, those necessary, simple things that, by the same token are all so much more unattainable now.

Friday 5th November

It is bonfire night. How silly would that sound to someone visiting earth.

I don't understand why more people don't see that Guy Fawkes was a genius. What better idea than to blow up the houses of parliament. And yes, with all those toe rags in it. I am being flippant but the modern day politician seems to be largely in it for their own pocket and their own piece of power. What happened to decent souls being there to serve their people and improve the overall country and its society?

Saturday 6th November

She won't make any contact with me at all anymore. She is so distant from me. How can I win her back? We were meant to be together, that much is obvious. Are the erosions of trust irreversible? *Darling, I didn't lie to you, the truth changed. I'll visit you in prison. I'll be the only one who stays true to you, is there for you.*

I must stop thinking and feeling like this. *She is gone, worse than that she is my foe. But our love was never gold plated, it was twenty-four carat.*

Sunday 7th November

Maybe it would have just been better if my wife had stayed. Maybe it would have all just been simpler. There was no magic, and I feel like I was at least mildly annoyed almost all of the time but just maybe, that would have been better than this? She was a nice woman.

Monday 8th November

She wrote me a letter today. In an envelope with a stamp. No return address though. I could smell her on the paper. She seems so adamant that I will not get her new phone number that she put pen to paper! I opened it with much trepidation and read it through splayed fingers. I read it, but have no interest in her attempt to cleanse her own soul. It was not a letter to me, more a cathartic act for her. *Well, I do hope you feel better princess.* She explained how much she enjoyed our relationship but that she can 'no longer entertain' being with me or being associated with me in any way. She said, 'I do not wish you lonely', yes, she actually used that phrase and then went onto say that she felt she didn't really know me until recently as she didn't like who I really was. She asked me never to get in touch again and said she won't write again. I won't reply. *But what if we accidently just bump into each other, my princess?*

I couldn't sleep as the words 'I do not wish you lonely' somehow hit the very depths of my soul and spun around and around in my head. I couldn't shake it. I wanted to cry, to cry out loud even but I knew that nobody would hear so there was not much point. And so, the sadness didn't come out. Am I grieving her or is this something else?

I wish my Dad was still alive. It's so long ago now since I have seen him, heard his voice or even just really seen what he looked like. I got out some old photos of him again and they made me cry a little. My memory of him, as with the memory of us all someday, is fading. *I can't allow her to tarnish it though.* Maybe I cannot even truly remember him, maybe my cloudy memory is idolising the father figure I needed, the father figure I yearn for today so much. I will choose my best photo of him and put it up on the wall so that I can see him, talk to him, every day. We all need a mentor, a guiding hand, and he was the nearest thing I ever had. Things could have been so different.

Tuesday 9th November

It can be such a difficult life. Such a difficult world to navigate. There are no moral compasses anymore. No leaders of men. The law was originally derived from what needed to be written down about what we knew collectively to be right to adhere to, but now it is just an instrument to see what people can get away with. New laws are now made and passed with that in mind. There is no one to look up to, there is no one to follow. The great leaders are all in the past. The great people tried and have now died. All the best ones are dead. Now, lies are the currency of true power. Once they are out there, they stick, gather and grow. Misinformation, disinformation, misdirection and who you can fool and in particular, how many, is the game. As we hurtle, we've become about individual advancement whilst forgetting our only advantage over other species was our ability to work together, to collaborate.

The robin reappeared today on my fence. Are they winter birds? It seemed to dance and sing all along my fence. It looked like it was putting on a performance just for me. Then it flew right next to the window where I was sitting. It came closer than ever before. It seemed to look me right in the eye and then it flew away.

No texts today from anyone, no emails and no post. I still somehow wished my Dad was here today. I want to talk to him, at least give him the chance to explain, to be my Dad again, the Dad I needed.

The police knocked on my front door mid-morning. They made a scene by parking right in front of my house with their flashing blue lights on. I did wonder what they might want, but more I wondered what they might know. They seem somewhat assertive in their posture. It's the curse of the leap year striking again. I really hope they don't look in my spare wheelie bin.

END